THE
CHRISTMAS LOG.

THE Christmas Log

THE

CHRISTMAS LOG.

A TALE

OF A FIRESIDE THAT HAD A GOOD GENIUS AND

A BAD ONE.

There are more things in heaven and on earth
That are dreamt of in our philosophy. — *Shakesper*

London:

E. LLOYD, 12, SALISBURY SQUARE.

LONDON:

PRINTED AND PUBLISHED BY E. LLOYD, SALISBURY SQUARE

PREFACE.

IN presenting to the public what it is hoped will be a highly seasonable little volume, the author has little more to say, than that his intention throughout the conduction of the story has been, not obtrusively, but in a pleasanter guise than moral saws usually present themselves, to inculcate a good principle.

The opinion that virtue need not be disagreeable, is an opinion that now has become fortunately sufficiently prevalent to insure a tolerably favourable reception to a work which puts truth in an agreeable light

The author has no wish or intention to deprecate criticism by pleading his well-meaning; but being of opinion that no book, large or small, ought to be without an object, he considers that in the outset he does but act candidly by proclaiming that he has one. That object is the exaltation of kind-heartedness and single-mindedness over chicanery, and those host of selfish feelings which some of our persons represented will exhibit.

Taking this view of the CHRISTMAS LOG, a somewhat higher claim of interest may be made for it, than were it merely put forth for the purpose of whiling away the tedium of some weary hour by a winter's fireside.

We hope that in what we intended to succeed in, we have succeeded in; but that is a question which the most admirable public will decide; and, *ad interim*, wishing all a " merry Christmas and a happy New Year," with all the usual addenda, we beg to introduce the CHRISTMAS LOG.

LONDON,
    December, 1846.

THE CHRISTMAS LOG.

CHAPTER the FIRST.

THE LEGACY.

IP! hip! hip! hurrah! Old Bootle is dead! Hip! hip! hip! hurrah! One cheer more—old Bootle is dead! There's a go—the old boy is dead! What do you think of that? There's a go!"

These words were uttered by Master Hannibal Jarvis, aged twenty-two, and about as incorrigible a puppy as

the good city of London could, in the year of grace, 1840, have
afforded to any naturalist who might be occupying his time in
looking for such specimens.

As he spoke, this young scion of the house of Jarvis dropped
the newspaper from his hand, the obituary of which had given
him the intelligence he had proclaimed in so uproarious a manner;
and, seizing the toast-rack that was on the breakfast-table, he
flourished it round his head in a most heroic fashion, until the last
remnant of toast hit his amiable sister, Miss Selina Jarvis, in the
near optic; whereupon, that young lady replevied, by throwing a
cup of chocolate in Hannibal's face.

"Now, now," cried Mr. Rhododenderon Jarvis—we like to give
his name in full—"now, now, children, don't let me have anything
of this sort.   Have not I often told you, that to stick together is
the only family motto.   Haven't I and my brother Sleekey stuck
together and made money?   Am I not a member of the common-
council; and when I go to a common hall——"

"A—a most uncommonly comman hall it is," said a voice; and
upon turning to look at the audacious speaker, Mr. Rhododenderon
saw that the invidious remark proceeded from the lips of Job
Brick, a lad of all-work, who, as an *attache* of the Jarvis family,
was, by dint of a little ingenuity, made uncommonly useful; for at
times he was a page, when Mrs. Jarvis saw company; and then
again, he became errand-boy to the drysaltery business—if we may
be allowed to use the term; and when Master Hannibal went out
in his father's one-horse chaise, Job Brick did the groom business;
and never would there have been such a pearl of a boy as Job, if
he had not had the failing—no uncommon one—of saying the
wrong thing exactly in the wrong place.

Not unfrequently had the anger of Mr. Jarvis—our readers will
remember his horticultural Christian name—been aroused to a
pitch bordering upon frenzy by some odd remark from Job, which
it would have required all the patience of his celebrated namesake
to bear.

"You rascal!" exclaimed Mr. Jarvis, "how dare you insult the
city of London in this way?"

" Yes, you low fellow," added Hannibal, " you take too many liberties."

" Always the way," chimed in Miss Selina, " with poor people; the more food you give them, the more insolent they are."

Sweet, amiable Selina! Go on, lovely specimen of that portion of creation which can be so near the angels, and so truly quite the other way. Go on cultivating that real fiend's vinegar disposition! Show yourself worthy—most eminently worthy of your parentage— and what Job Brick would have called your " broughtings up."

" The world is an unweeded garden ;
Things rank and gross in nature possess it merely "—

and therefore, you are in the fashion, dear Selina.

" I tell you what it is, Mr. J., said the illustrious mother; " I tell you what it is, if you put up with that boy's impertinence, I won't, that's all."

" Lor!" said Job, " what have I done, I should like to know, that you all set upon me. Isn't a fellow all for to go to say nothink no how?"

" Not a word—not a word!" exclaimed Mr. Jarvis. " And now, my dear Hannibal, what do you mean?' Is old Bootle really dead?"

' Yes—oh! yes. Leastways it's here in the paper, ma. Hear you :—' At Bootle Hall, Wilts, suddenly, Jeremiah Bootle, Esq., sincerely regretted. His end was peace.' I believe there's no mistake about that, at all events. It's his name as pat as nine-pence, you see, and Wilts is his county. What a go, aint it?"

" But—but," said Mr. Jarvis, as he wiped the perspiration from his brow; " but we—don't know, you know. It's a fact that the old man did say he would leave us everything; but we don't know, you know. Bless me, I'm all over of a tremble like—like——"

" A pickpocket caught in the blessed fact," said Job.

This was flagrant; and Mr. Jarvis shook his clenched hand at Job, as he muttered, ' If my feelings were not so—so very much cut up at the death of my much respected wife's uncle, Mr. Bootle, I'd—I'd—but no matter. You rascal, you have no more feeling than a blacking-brush."

Job looked as vacantly stupid as it was possible for any human being to look. He always did when he had said anything peculiarly uncomfortable to the Jarvis's. An odd boy was Job Brick— a very odd boy.

" The death of the much respected Mr. Bootle," said Rhododenderon Jarvis. "awakens a crowd of—a—a—feelings, I may say, and associations. If he has left his money to somebody else, my dears, than to us, we cannot be supposed to—to feel that he has acted judiciously ; but if, on the contrary——"

" Oh, bother !" cried the filial Hannibal. " You aint at the common council now, father. If the old buffer has not left us all his tin, hang him if I put on an inch of crape for him ; and, if he has, won't we come it rather this season, I believe you ! I think the Trucots and the Lupins will look a little blue, mother."

" I think, my dear," replied Mrs. Jarvis, "that it will be quite necessary we shouldn't know such people as the Trucots and the Lupins. I should say go westward—westward at once, among the real nobs, you know. Only think of a town chariot and a drive in the parks ! I declare I hate the very sound of the drysalting business. Pah ! It's most odious. Then a country box—of course we will have a country box—and then——"

" What a lot of chickens we shall have when they are all hatched !" said Job, in an affectedly abstracted manner, looking up to the ceiling.

The remark was not lost upon those who heard it ; and had it not been that, from long habit, the Jarvis's family were used to such little asides from Job, and likewise knew that some solid advantages accrued from having him in their service—for he came at small wages and did a world of work—they would have resented his intrusive philosophy by showing him the door-step. But that was an extreme measure which, under the circumstances, they did not feel inclined to indulge in ; so Job once more escaped the consequences of his rashness.

Perhaps, too, Mr. Jarvis himself thought there was something in the shape of sound philosophy in the remark that Job had made ; for he himself expressed it in a different shape.

" Well, well," he said, " of course we can't know exactly what's done and what aint in the matter. We certainly have had the comfortable assurance from Mr. Bootle that he did intend to leave us everything, I must say ; and, as we have seen his death in the public papers, I think we ought to send for—" here Mr. Jarvis lowered his voice and glanced towards Job, who who was dusting a glass on the side-board, before he added—" Cousin Bloomenback. Eh ! my dear?"

" Certainly," said Mrs. Jarvis. " We all know that if anybody can manage anything, Cousin Bloomenback, attorney-at-law, is the man. He is my cousin eleven times removed ; but it shows what talent there is in the Bloomenback's, and what a fortunate man you are, Mr. Rhododenderon Jarvis."

" I know that, my dear ; and, therefore, I say, in this junc;-ture send for Cousin Bloomenback at once. He will know how to prosecute."

" I believe you," said Job. " Innocent or guilty, it's all the same to him."

" Never mind him, my dear ; we will get rid of him soon. I was about to say that Mr. Bloomenback will know how to prosecute the necessary inquiries, so send for him at once. You, Hannibal, go, and you can take the newspaper with you, you know."

" Very good," said Hannibal. " I have no sort of objections ; I dare say it's all right enough. All I stipulate for is, that you cut the business, father. They do say that old Bootle is worth a hundred thousand pounds. There will be a haul ; upon my life, I feel quite nobbish already. Mind, I'm to have my private cab and tiger—you understand. Egad, won't I come it ! I will let them see what Bishopsgate-within can do ; shooting—hunting—driving—racing—boating. Oh ! what glorious fun and as for the gals——"

" Hannibal," said Mrs. Jarvis, " how dare you?"

" Well, I didn't say anything, mother."

" And he'll do less," said Job.

" I tell you what it is, my fine fellow," said Hannibal to Job, " you have been too long with us, and that's a fact ; you are an mpertinent scoundrel."

" Well," said Job, " he's willing to go.   Mrs. Lupin has such a lot o' gals.   She wants a boy, she says, and she's offered to take me.   Won't she be amused when I tells her all I knows about what I knows."

" Silence ! you—you rascal," cried Mr. Jarvis, for he seemed to be under some apprehensions of Job.

" Yes, yes, silence," stammered Hannibal, " we—we will forgive you this once."

" Job, you are a very good lad when you like," said Mrs. Jarvis, in a fidgetty manner ; " but really you do try one's patience too much—you know you do.   Howsomdever, we won't say any more about it."

" Job," said Selina, " you'd have been turned away, you know, many a time if it hadn't been for me—you know that."

The only reply Job ventured to all these conciliatory speeches was, in a low tone, to whistle a tune, and then, having finished polishing the glass he had been about, he gave a sort of circular nod as he came to the few last notes of the popular air he was executing, and left the room.

It is quite clear that the Jarvis's dare not turn Job away.   How very extraordinary that such good people should be afraid of their boy-of-all-work.   Job must know something.   Is it a family secret, or have each of the Jarvis's a something they dread a discovery of, but which Job knows, and so keeps them all in chains ?   We shall see shortly.

When he had left the room, there was an uncomfortable sort of pause of a few moments duration, which was, however, at length broken by Mrs. Jarvis, saying,—

" Well, my dear, you may as well go to Mr. Bloomenback's at once."

" Yes, I'm going ; I suppose I may ride.   It's a deuce of a way, you know, to New Inn."

As he made this remark, he held out his hand, and, after some rummaging, his mother graciously placed a shilling in it, saying, as she did so,—

" There's for two omnibuses, Hannibal ; and tell Mr. Bloomenback we shall be glad to see him to take a bit of dinner with us to-day, and then we can talk over the affair quite comfortably with him. Oh! he's a remarkably clever man, he is, as we know, don't we, Mr. J.?"

"Yes, yes," said Rhododenderon, rather impatiently; "we know all about that. But you be off, Hannibal. Take the newspaper with you, and don't lose any more time. Be off with you, and be sure you bring Mr. Bloomenback with you. Of course, I'll stand all charges; and if he likes a cab better than the omnibus, don't make any objection. You know his number—3, New Inn. How very nervous I am, to be sure. Really I—I haven't been so agitated since they wouldn't have me for sheriff."

Hannibal left the house to proceed on his errand to New Inn, but he had not been gone five minutes when Job Brick flung open the breakfast-parlour-door, and announced,—

"Mr. Gage."

———

CHAPTER II.

GREAT CHANGES.

THIS most abrupt announcement of a name perfectly unknown to the Jarvis family took them by surprise, and produced all that amount of consternation which the sudden arrival of any stranger always does produce in a vulgar, fussy family.

"Mr. Gage!" exclaimed Rhododenderon Jarvis—"Mr. Gage! I don't know him. Really now—ahem! Upon my word I don't know the gentleman. Your servant, sir; you have the advantage of me, really."

"Excuse me, sir, and you ladies," said a gentlemanly-looking and rather elderly gentleman, as he entered the apartment, "I feel that I owe you many apologies for this seemingly uncourteous intrusion, although it is not such in reality. Pray, have I the honour of addressing Mr. Rhododenderon Jarvis?"

"That is my name, sir."

"Thank you, sir; thank you, madam. I hope you accept of my apologies; and you, young lady, who, if you be as amiable as you are beautiful, I'm sure I shall not plead to in vain."

Miss Selina Jarvis had never had such a compliment paid to her in all her life before. She was perfectly enchanted, and put on such an amiable simper, that all her mouthful of bad teeth was exhibited at once, and Mrs. Jarvis, although the stranger had paid her no direct compliment in words, had, by his manner, implied one, looked quite pleased, and bridled up with an expression of intense satisfaction. Moreover, Mr. Gage had asked Mr. Jarvis if he had the honour of addressing him. He could not have said more had he been doubtful of the identity of a Lord Mayor.

"Pray be seated, sir," said Jarvis; "I'm quite sure—ahem! —that any business you may come about may be arranged with much satisfaction; you are so much the gentleman."

"Oh, very!" said Selina.

"Quite, quite," cried Mrs. Jarvis, and Mr. Gage bowed his head like a Mandarin to the compliments that were showered upon him.

"Ladies," he said, with a sigh, "and you, Mr. Jarvis, I come on a melancholy errand—a very melancholy errand. For the last twenty years I have had the honour and the satisfaction to be the legal adviser of Jeremiah Bootle, Esq., of Wilts. I grieve now to say that that gentleman is no more."

Jarvis glanced at his wife and daughter, as much as to say, "Had we not better plead ignorance?" and a slight nod from the female Jarvis's decided him in the policy of so doing.

"No more," he exclaimed, "no more! Dear, dear! Is it possible? Poor old Mr. Bootle! Well, I am sorry! Respectable, comfortable old gentleman! How many will miss you, and regret you! So Mr. Bootle is dead, is he? Well, well, that's the way; we are all hearing continually of somebody popping off. How true it is that we are here to-day and gone to-morrow!"

"It is remarkably true, Mr. Jarvis, but you will not suppose that I merely came here from my chambers in Lincoln's Inn to announce to you a death, and although what I am going to say to you, I know, will not lessen your grief in the least, yet it is quite necessary that I should say it."

" Pray, sir—go—on," gasped Rhododenderon Jarvis.

" Old Mr. Bootle, then, has died immensely rich, and he has left all to you and your most exemplary family—one hundred and fifty thousand pounds in India stock and English funds; sixty thousand in Dutch Securities; four estates, two of them with manorial rights and privileges; personal property to the tune of twenty-five thousand pounds."

" Stop, stop !" gasped Jarvis, as Mrs. J. uttered quite a shriek, and Selina looked as if she was reasoning with herself upon the propriety of fainting. " Stop, stop—you—you don't mean to say that—that it's all left to us ?"

" Every sixpence."

" The—the estates—the—manorial rights—the personals—the funded property—my head is going round and round like a humming top. Say it again, Mr. Greengage—you don't mean it ?"

" My name is Gage, sir, without the green. Nobody ever thought me green in all my life; and now that I have told you what you are possessed of, allow me to describe to you my last interview with poor old Mr. Bootle, who, I believe, stands in the relationship of uncle to Mrs. Jarvis."

" Yes, that is the relationship," gasped Mrs. Jarvis. " Oh! good gracious! what laces—what satins—what feathers—what diamonds I am thoroughly bewildered, Mr. what's-your-name, are you quite sure? There can be no mistake, I hope; that would be dreadful."

" Mistake!" screamed Selina, " oh, good gracious ! I should never get out of my bed again if there was."

" Ladies, you may be perfectly assured of the facts as I relate them to you. There is no mistake, and can be none; and now I pray you to do me the favour of attending to what I have to say to you. About three months ago, I saw Mr. Bootle, and had a long and deeply interesting interview with that old gentleman, upon family affairs. The particulars of that interview I shall now relate to you, as I feel it is my duty to do so now, considering the situation in which you stand with regard to the property."

The ladies had been about to leave the room, but their curiosity was now so strongly excited by what Mr. Gage said, that they could not think of doing so, but composed themselves to listen.

"You are doubtless aware, " commenced Mr. Gage, "that the old age of Mr. Bootle was much embittered by family discords. You know that he married late in life, and that that union was, what he considered, blessed by the birth of a daughter, whom he named Lucinda, after her mother, who expired three days after the infant's birth."

"Oh! yes, yes," said Mrs. Jarvis, rather impatiently.

"The little child then became all the care of the old man, but thrived for all that, and grew a handsome girl, as perhaps you know quite well already, for Lucinda Bootle was famed for her beauty throughout the whole county of Wilts; and it was a sweet thing to see her at the age of sixteen walking with her father, who was then nearly sixty, and the old man looking so proud and delighted with his child, that everybody envied him so much happiness. But, perhaps, you know all that."

The Jarvis's were evidently very uneasy during this exordium of the attorney's, and they looked as if they would fain have said, "Drop all the sentimental, if you please, and go on." But Mr. Gage was determined to tell the story in his own way, so he proceeded, much to the evident annoyance of the Jarvis's.

"There were many people who said, when they saw how happy the old man and his child was, that it could not last, and just about that time, you, all of you, found him out, and made him aware of those claims of relationship, which distance and some little family bickerings had for years lain in abeyance. He received you well enough, as you all know, and, when he came to London, you treated him, as he himself told me, most kindly."

"We did," said Jarvis, drawing a long breath—"we did. It was as well our duty as our inclination so to do."

"Agreed. And the old man appreciated the kindness. You found that he had got a promise from his daughter, that she would not marry while he lived; and you found out that she was attached to a Lieutenant Brotherton, a very bad character, I think, you found out he was."

"Ye—ye—yes," said Rhododenderon Jarvis, faintly.

"Good. The consequence of all that was, that the old man forbade Brotherton his house, and then, that his child flung herself at his feet, and told him she was already a wife. The father was seized with illness, and before he entirely recovered, you satisfactorily proved to him, that his daughter was but the mistress of Brotherton, who had a wife already, residing in the city of London; and then, Mr. Bootle discarded her for ever from his heart; and, seven years ago, retired to his country seat, in Wilts, seeing no one, but shutting himself up completely from the world, and entertaining a good opinion of no one but you, and your family, suffering nobody to wait upon him but an old gardener, who had been in his service many years; for although there was a woman servant, a daughter of the gardener in the house, old Mr. Bootle would never suffer her to come near him, and only consented to her being there on condition, that she never crossed his path."

"We have heard all that."

"Exactly. Well, it is only lately that the old man has found that his daughter, Lucinda, became a mother, and that she herself was no more."

"Is she dead?" said Jarvis, "you are sure Lucinda is dead?'

"To all the world, most completely," replied Mr. Gage; "but she has a daughter now at boarding school, near London, utterly and entirely destitute—that is to say, she is dependent upon you completely; and I will tell you exactly what old Mr. Bootle said to me about it when last I saw him, and communicated to him the fact of his daughter's death. 'Mr. Gage,' he said, 'mention her more to me. All I have in the world. I shall leave to the Jarvis's, for they saved me from being grossly deceived by my own flesh and blood; but—but—' and then his voice faltered as he spoke—'the child is innocent.' "

"Yes," interposed Selina, "but there's no knowing—what's bred in the bone, you know, will never come out of the flesh.'

"Well, then," said Rhododenderon Jarvis, "we will hear all that this gentleman has to say."

"Thank you," said the lawyer, with a slight tone of sarcasm—

" thank you. Without at all entering into the question of whether or not vice is hereditary, I will proceed. The child's name is Marianna. And Mr. Bootle concluded his remarks concerning it, by saying to me,—

" ' I cannot, Mr. Gage, bring myself to name that offspring of disgrace in my will, but I leave a memorandum in the Jarvis' family, to do what is necessary for it—I leave most emphatically, my child's child to the generosity of the people to whom I leave all my property."

" Oh !" said Jarvis.

" Dear me," said Mrs. Jarvis.

" Yes," added Mr. Gage, " those were his precise words, and therefore, it has become a paramount duty on my part, to repeat them."

" But—but," interposed Jarvis, " where is the father ? "

" Dead—killed in the battle of Bhoopatrafutumble, in India ! "

" God bless me!" said Mrs. Javies. " And so this Marianna is at school—I wonder if there is much owing."

" That I don't know. But you will see what a great duty you have to do, in the way of providing for this child, now six years of age ; you will find that all is left to you, and out of such abundance you can bestow a fortune easily upon Marianna ; I should recommend you to be very liberal."

" A fortune ! " exclaimed Javris. " Well, really I—I don't know about that exactly. A fortune indeed ! why, you see, Mr. Gage, we are placed in a very delicate position as regards this orphan girl ; our great respect for the feelings, the wishes, and the intentions of our deceased relative, Mr. Bootle, will not permit us to do what we otherwise might do. If he had wished Marianna Brotherton, for that is I suppose what we must call her, to have a fortune, he could easily have left her one, you see."

" Oh, no doubt ! "

" But as he did not do so, it seems to me, Mr. Gage, that he could not possibly mean any such thing, so, notwithstanding we should, of course, be inclined to do all that you say, we owe so much to the deceased Mr. Bootle, that we dare not."

"Mr. Jarvis, of course you have full power to do, or not to do, just what you please; you are a very wealthy man now; you are, in fact, one of the wealthiest commoners in this country, and can please yourself: I only ventured to advise you in the matter, knowing old Mr. Bootle's feelings."

"Oh! there's no blame to you, Mr. what's-your-name," said Mrs. Jarvis, with a toss of her head; "only when people speak of giving away a fortune, it's enough to make people speak out."

"Do not mistake me," said Mr. Gage, "I did not by any means wish you to give up the bulk of Mr. Bootle's property; I only thought, for instance, that if you were to settle five hundred pounds per annum on Marianna."

"What!" exclaimed Jarvis, "five hundred pounds did you say —five hundred?"

"Yes. But large as that sum may sound, you will be pleased to recollect that your income from Mr. Bootle's property will really, with the most ordinary management, be somewhere about fifteen thousand pounds per annum; so I thought you might as well manage to let Marianna, whom the old man thought he was amply providing for, by leaving her to your generosity, have a thirtieth of that sum. Poor thing! she cannot help her misfortunes. I am not myself in possession of the various circumstances that went to prove that Lucinda was not married to Brotherton—I am forced to take that for granted. But be that how it may, still you will admit that the child, Marianna, has nothing to do with it."

"Well, well, sir, we will think about it," said Jarvis, who no more thought of giving Marianna five hundred pounds per annum, than of giving her the whole of her grandfather's property. "We will think of it, and in the meantime, I am of course anxious to take the necessary steps that will place me in possession of Mr. Bootle's property."

"That will take some time," said Mr. Gage. "I have not the will."

"Not the will?"

"No; it is in the possession of a gentleman of the legal profession, who is now abroad on a commission to collect evidence in

a very complicated case.   I drew up the will though, and know its
purport.   It is as short as simplicity of purpose can make it; and
simply leaves all to you and your heirs, without limitation, except
as regards the payment of any just debts that may be due by him
at the time of his demise."

"But—but that's awkward—when will the party be back?"

"In a month.   And, in the interim, I am in a position to hand
to you any cash you wish to have on your own note-of-hand, payable
in the period I have named.   I am quite satisfied with my security, Mr. Jarvis."

There can be no mistake about it now, thought the drysalter.
When a lawyer offers to advance you money, you may be sure
euough that all is right.   Oh, yes, there is no mistake now.

"Sir, I thank you.   Do you think I could have—say five
thousand pounds?"

"Ten thousand if you like, Mr. Jarvis."

"No, no, I don't want money exactly; but still a month is long
to wait, and five thousand would be an accommodation.'

"You shall have a cheque for the amount to-morrow on your
promissory note."

Mr. Jarvis now, for the first time, seemed really to be over-
whelmed with an idea of his own good fortune, and he turned so
pale, that his wife recommended a stimulant in the shape of a glass
of brandy, which was duly swallowed, and produced a reviving
effect upon him, after which, Mr. Gage rose, saying,—

"I have now, sir, discharged my errand, and will await upon
you again to-morrow, if you please; and if you are not actually
provided with a man of business, I need not say that of course
I shall be very happy to———"

"Oh, yes, we are,' interrupted Mrs. Jarvis; "Mr. Bloomenback of New Inn, conducts all our law matters;—and a clever
man he is."

"No doubt, madam, no doubt.   I shall leave you in his hands
with great pleasure.   I think, as well as I recollect, that
gentleman was instrumental in getting up the evidence that
convinced old Mr. Bootle of his daughter's bad conduct."

"That bad conduct, sir," said Jarvis, "was a melancholy fact; and therefore, there needed no one to be instrumental in getting up anything about it. Mr. Bloomenback is a very clever practitioner indeed—a distant connection of Mrs. Jarvis's. We respect him highly."

"No doubt, sir, no doubt. I now take my leave of you, again urging you, as a friend, to take the case of young Marianna Brotherton into your serious consideration. You can well afford to do a liberal thing as regards her, which, in the opinions of all persons, must redound greatly to your advantage, you may depend."

"Sir," said the drysalter, haughtily, "men of property do not like to be dictated to, I can assure you. Men of fifteen thousand pounds per annum form their own conclusions. Good morning, sir, good morning."

Mr. Gage bowed himself out, after receiving a very supercilious and slight inclination of the head from the ladies, who thought likewise, that women of fifteen thousand pounds per annum might just as well be impertinent and unlady-like. Lady-like, do we say, when even Mrs. and Miss Jarvis, coldly selfish and unfeelingly arrogant as they both were, were entitled to that large amount of commendation.

Alas, poor Marianna Brotherton, we pity thee!

CHAPTER III.

THE ATTORNEY IN NEW INN.

WHILE all this was going on at the house of the Jarvis's, Master Hannibal was making his way to New Inn. To those acquainted with that locality, we need say nothing of the delights of that legal Coventry, New Inn; but to these who are unacquainted with the place and its localities, it may be worth while to state, that a more dingy, despicable hole does not exist throughout the metropolis.

It is the h   ndecayed lawyers—men who have never either

reached respectability in their profession, or have sadly fallen off from that high and palmy state.

We do not use this term respectability invidiously, to signify that those members of the legal profession who luxuriate in New Inn are worse than their fellows in more highly favoured situations, but we use the term in its strictly legal sense, a respectable man in the profession being one who has high and costly practice, thus establishing the converge of the proposition, that a man who has little to do, and that little of a pettifogging and cheap character, cannot be respectable.

And as it always happens that poverty pays more largely for the accommodations it requires, it is found that, in New Inn, if a set of chambers, of the annual value of twelve pounds, be to let, the applicant for them must not only undergo a rigorous examination before a pompous official in a dirty room, to which he is introduced by the inn porter; but, if he be declared to be sufficiently perfect to be admitted as a resident within the dirty precincts, he is required to pay two guineas to the aforesaid pompous and scarcely civil official for the gratifying information.

It was towards this luxurious retreat, in which, if any one wishes to bring himself to contemplate suicide as a great relief, he had better reside six months, that Hannibal Jarvis bent his steps.

It was in the natural order and fitness of things that Mr. Bloomenback should reside in such a dingy place and in the dingiest corner of it; his deeds were not exactly of a character congenial to daylight, and, although he always flattered himself that the day would come when he would make a dashing use of the wealth he had been accumulating, he still lived and crept about the precincts of New Inn, hoarding and amassing that gold which his craven spirit never permitted him to enjoy.

He was a tall, wiry-looking man, with iron-grey hair; there was a keen and sinister expression about his eyes, rather assisted by the fact of a slight obliquity of vision, which made his clients doubtful, at times, if he were looking at them or through the dingy window panes at the inn pump.

Nothing came amiss to Bloomenback; his patience, too, was inexhaustible—no spider ever spun his web, and then retired to some distant corner, to watch the result of his machinations, with greater philosophy than did Mr. Bloomenback lay the train for some event and then await its coming.

The young heir apparent, as he conceived himself to be, to fifteen thousand pounds a year, marched into New Inn with an air and manner which seemed to say, how much he considered his dignity to be compromised by being seen in such a place; and, although he felt the consciousness that no one as yet knew of his great exaltation, he dived into the narrow door-way, leading to Bloomenback's chambers, with a degree of satisfaction that he was out of the daylight.

A smart rap at the chamber door, brought out the great Bloomenback in person, who made his appearance, as was his custom, with a pen in his mouth; and when he saw who his visitor was, he removed that professional looking insignia, and with a chuckle, exclaimed,—

"Oh! of course; I knew it—I knew some of you would be here this morning. Come in; old Bootle is dead—you have found that out of course. Well, what follows; is all right?

"Let me take breath," said Hannibal Jarvis; "of all the infernal pestiferous places for a man to live in, this is about the worst; upon my life, I couldn't bear it long."

"Oh! indeed!—you need say no more, it requires no conjuror to tell the prosperous man from the disappointed one. We have succeeded."

"We! I don't know what you mean by we—I really can't tell what you are driving at, Bloomenback. The governor wants to see you, all that we knew is, that old Bootle is dead, and that it was always supposed he would cut up for about fifteen thousand a year; and that when he died, we should come in for a tolerable share, if not for all."

" And then, there is a certain promissory note, is there not, to be filled up with half a year's income. You seem to forget that Mr. Hannibal Jarvis."

"Now, you don't mean to say, Mr. Bloomenback, that you would have the coolness to expect seven thousand five hundred pounds for your share in the business?"

"Bah!" said Mr. Bloomenback, "I don't deal with boys; your father's the man for me; we understand each other, and tell him, that within an hour, I shall be in Bishopsgate. I know the attorneys well of the late Mr. Bootle; we had better be quiet, for they will lose no time in communicating with you if it be necessary; if you hear nothing from them, you can hope for nothing, and then there is only one resource left."

"What? there is a resource then."

"Go away—go away; I am busy. All will be done that is necesaary; we shall see the colour of old Bootle's money, although perhaps not so much as it would be gratifying to be dazzled with. Be off with you—be off with you; hush—there's a knock. I have now and then a queer client or two, who don't exactly choose to meet anybody in my chambers; so step into yon inner room, you shall not be imprisoned long, and if you are, there is one of the finest views, from the window, of a pump out of repair and the dust-hole and sink, belonging to No. 3, that you can imagine; you may fancy it some beautiful place on the Rhine, if your imagination be strong enough."

"Oh, thank you, the Rhine indeed; the deuce take your queer clients that are afraid to meet anybody; I will say that, of all the dung-holes in the world, that ever I was in, your chambers are the worst."

The further grumblings of young Jarvis were put a stop to by the shutting of the door in his face; and when Mr. Bloomenback answered the summons for admission, made by the new comer, he was surprised to find that it was no other than Mr. Jarvis himself, who after a little reflection, when Mr. Gage had left him, had thought it desirable to take a cab and run down to New Inn at once, to see Bloomenback.

He had been more prompted to this course by his impatience than his reason, for he could not doubt that the lawyer would visit him; but then the communication of Mr. Gage was of so startling a character, and had put him into such a state of perturbation and agitation, that physical exercise was absolutely necessary to get rid of the excitement.

" My good friend Jarvis," said Bloomenback ; " am I indeed so honoured ; ah ! I perceive you have intelligence of moment, but I knew it beforehand."

" You do not know it all. I suppose Hannibal has been here, but he knows not further than the death of Bootle. Give me a seat—give me a seat, Bloomenback, and you shall know all; we always expected something, but we did not look for such complete success—I say, complete success : you understand what that means."

" I ought. Old Bootle has left you a large legacy."

" No; he has left no legacy to any human being; we have everything."

There was a slightly increased colour upon the face of Bloomenback as he heard these words, and then he seemed to recollect that Hannibal was in the next apartment, and he said at once,—

" Your son is here. Not knowing who it might be that was at my chamber's-door, I got him to walk into the next room; if you have any objection to him as an auditor there he remains; if not, it's as well to call him at once."

" With this proviso," said Jarvis, " that you say nothing further to him of our private arrangements. You must dine with us to-day, and you and I must find some opportunity for an hour's calm converse. I have seen Gage, the old man's attorney."

" And do you mean to tell me," said Mr. Bloomenback, as he rose to liberate Hannibal, " do you mean to tell me that it was from him that you had the news of everything being left you."

" I do ; and coming, therefore, from such a quarter it may be relied on; but, as you know, we have yet our perplexities."

" True, true, most true; and if my advice had been taken—"

" Hush ! No more at present; after dinner we will speak."

The attorney, with a strange smile upon his face, liberated Hannibal, whose countenance fell when he saw it was his father, for he feared that something had occurred which had induced him to come and countermand the invitation to Bloomenback; a second glance, however, at the countenance of his exemplary parent was sufficient to convince him that such was not the case, and when his father said, " Well, Hannibal, old Bootle has left us everything," a sort of faintness came over young Jarvis, and he was forced to sit down, as he gasped out,—

" You—you don't mean that, governor, do you? I'll serve out a few people if it is the case. How much am I to have? You spoke of a pump, Bloomenback; a drop of water would not be amiss. I feel as queer as possible with the sudden surprise."

" No water," said Bloomenback, as he went to a cupboard and produced a black bottle and a glass without a leg—" no water, my good friends—no water. It does so happen sometimes that in the still hours of the night—for I sleep here, you know—an uncomfortable feeling creeps over me. I fancy that the air is hot and thick, and now and then that strange eyes are peeping at me between the bed-curtains; then I find this, my friends. '

" Ah!" said young Jarvis, " and you swallow him up as you do most of your friends. That's not bad, is it Bloomenback?"

" Not at all," said the lawyer, as he gave Hannibal a tap on the head with the bottle, that was a great deal too hard to be pleasant or encouraging, " not at all bad. I suppose you mean now to be a brick, and a sort of man about town—to frequent taverns—drive your horses on footpaths—wrench off knockers, and make yourself otherwise a distinguished personage."

" That may be all very well," said young Jarvis, " but flint glass is not the pleasantest thing in the world to knock anybody's head with."

Mr. Bloomenback only smiled as he filled a glass of strong brandy from the suspicious looking bottle to each of his guests, and then took care to put them in countenance by swallowing one himself with a *gout* that showed he was not altogether unused to that gentle stimulant.

" What is to be done?" said young Hannibal, " how are we to get the money?"

" Don't attempt to get it—do nothing," said Bloomenback;

"leave the whole affair in the hands of Mr. Bootle's solicitors; it will be as well not even to mention my existence."

"I am afraid that has been done already," said Jarvis; "and to-morrow I am offered five thousand pounds in advance if I want it; as, in consequence of the absence of a party on the continent, in whose hands the will was deposited, it may be a month before the affair can be properly arranged."

"Indeed!" said Bloomenback; "I don't like that, and yet you say that Messrs. Gage and Co. offer you five thousand pounds as an advance; surely all must be right—quite right; they are not the firm to do a thing of that sort, unless, they know well the ground they are treading on. Take it, I say by all means—by all means take it.'

"My own inclination goes that way."

"And mine—and mine. I want a thousand pounds for a particular purpose."

Jarvis looked at Bloomenback for a moment, as if it were quite incomprehensible to him that there could be such an amount of impertinence in any human being, and then he said in a low voice,—

"We will talk of that after dinner, Mr. Bloomenback; at present we can come to no precise conclusion; the vehicle that brought me down here is in the Strand; are you willing to come with me at once?"

"I am quite willing," said the lawyer; and the three, than whom, perhaps, there could not have been found three greater rogues in London, left the place.

The agitation of the elder Jarvis was really painfully apparent; it seemed as if now, that he knew himself the possessor of fifteen thousand a year, the principal troubles of his existence, had begun; but how had he achieved that result? by what means had he attained to that fancied elevation?—fearful questions to Rhododenderon Jarvis.

CHAPTER IV.

THE OLD HOUSEKEEPER.

WHILE these things were going on in London, there was one portion of the county of Wilts, wherein there was a considerable amount of agitation of hopes, fears, wishes, and even tears.

These symptoms of humanity were to be found in an old mansion called the Priory, which was certainly, as well as the most ancient, one of the most beautiful country seats in the whole county.

It was replete with all those sights and associations which make such places charming resting spots for the mind as well as for the body; the rich growth of wood, much of it a century in age, spoke magnificently of the past, and lent to the whole estate an air of melancholy grandeur which, while it might, to some extent, have a saddening influence on the mind, could not but encourage and call into active existence some of its higher qualities.

There were long corridors, ancient apartments, panelled chambers, stately galleries, a chapel, and all the thousand and one odd nooks and corners, which are to be found in those ancient English houses, the owners of which were wont to consider hospitality as the king of virtues.

And this was the place, which, once upon a time, had been the scene of much happiness, notwithstanding, it seemed an ill-assorted union for Mr. Bootle, its proprietor, at the mature age of three or four and forty, to unite himself to a young and blooming girl of about half that age.

To them, however, the disparity of mere duration of time, was as nothing, for never did lover with a more ardent devotion, look upon the face of one dear to him, than did Mr. Bootle upon the blooming countenance of the beautiful Lucinda.

And had he not, to the full, entitled himself to all the veneration of affection, with which she could regard him? he had soothed the last moments of a parent dear to her beyond all ordinary tenderness—he had laid in an honoured grave, the only being who had held her to the world, by the ties of fond affection, and was it to be wondered at, that that innocent and beautiful girl should cling, without regard to whether he were a year older or a year younger than romance might consider the beau ideal of a lover's age, to one to whom she owed so much.

While she pleased, she had a happy and a secure home at the Priory, and not even the busy tongue of seldom-failing slander could attack the fair fame of Lucinda Deverel.

It was true enough that the gossips, when it was formally announced from the pulpit of the parish church, that if nobody had anything to say to the contrary, Lucinda Deverel would certainly become Mrs. Bootle—that they knew how it would be; that there was no fool like an old fool, and a variety of other complimentary expressions; but for all that, the happiness of the married couple was like the sunlight overcoming all obstacles, and lending the radiance of its beauty to the landscape of their affections, despite all that detractors ever felt or ever thought.

The time passed pleasantly, and all was merry as a marriage-bell till the young mother sank into her grave, leaving her first-born, a shivering infant, in its father's arms; and then the old man—for old he became in spirit, though not in years—battled for long with his mighty grief, and it was not until he was told the infant was growing in strength and beauty, as well as in similitude to her whom he had lost, that a calm spirit came over him, and he began to look around him upon the scenes he used to love.

Time, the great conqueror of grief, at length had its usual effect; the grief that had been loud, even almost to madness, wept itself to sleep; and on calm summer eves, Mr. Bootle would walk out, holding his little daughter by the hand, and speaking to her with a chastened and gentle spirit of that mother who had long left her, seemingly for the cold obstruction of the grave, but really for that home which is eternal, beneath brighter skies than the fancy of poets or the skill of painters ever depicted.

He lived a simple and a frugal life, leaving his vast income to accumulate, until all said that the young child would be the

richest heiress England could boast; and so it grew in beauty
and intelligence, until sixteen summers had passed away.

From the few slight words which had fallen during Mr. Gage's
conversation with the Jarvis' family, we may guess the rest
without recapitulation; and now taking up the thread of our
narrative on that same morning when Hannibal Jarvis had shouted
out so gaily, that old Bootle was dead, we beg to introduce the
reader to what was called the rose-panelled chamber of the
Priory.

And here we may prepare our friends for a surprise; and
when those who have followed us thus far in our narrative, hear
Mr. Bootle saying something, it may look a little discrepant with
the former statement of his death, but, perhaps, if we listen
attentively to what he does say, we may be let into the secret.

He is not one of those moody, muttering persons, sacred to melodramas and lunatic novels, who make long speeches to silence and to loneliness, but he has a substantial listener in the shape of Mrs. Green, his housekeeper, who has been with him for many a long year, and who has seen the rise and fall, and then again the partial rise of his happiness.

Mrs. Green was one of those rare personages who, without sinister motives, and without one wish beyond doing her duty in her situation, had acquired, from sheer force of desert, a great influence over her master. She had not opposed his marriage when he told her that it was a step, he thought, would make him a happier man; and his young wife had found in her as kind and cheerful a companion as if she had chosen her herself.

"Mr. Bootle," said Mrs. Green, "it's of no mortal use you're being as nervous as a fiddlestick, since I've come back to you after your melancholies; when you wouldn't have a female in the place for six months, you know you have been something like yourself again."

"But can you wonder at my being nervous, and in a state of intense excitement, when you consider the importance of the stake I am now playing for—when you consider, Mrs. Green, that I'm trying to see if the people upon whom I bestowed my greatest affections, have really the smallest regard for me? you know what a passion Mr. Gage has put me in; you know that a man of prejudice would have been angry at the pains the Jarvises took to convince me of what was true; but I conquered that feeling, and now, to be told that they would behave basely, that they would take all I gave, and that my best and last wishes would be repudiated——"

"Ah," said Mrs. Green, "you're a poor old soul, and don't know much of the world yet. Mr. Gage knows them well enough, or else he is not the sort of person to have said all he did say."

"He would have said too much—too much."

"Indeed, Mr. Bootle, he would not have said too much. All he wanted to say was, that the Jarvises had made the worst of everything, and you know well enough that they did so."

C

"Oh! no, no, no! Mr. Jarvis wept, actually wept. I saw his tears, when he gave me the evidence of my child's dishonour—dishonour horrible to know, and yet a truth—yes, a truth, which ought not to have been hidden from me. I say again that I am not one who will cast blame upon a messenger, because he happens to bring evil tidings. I tell you, I saw Jarvis weep."

"Weep, indeed! Are you so foolish, Mr. Bootle, as to think there's anything in that? Weep—a fiddlestick! of course he can weep."

"He did more: he begged and prayed of me to have some consideration for even my guilty child. It was he whom I nearly quarrelled with, for urging me to forgive her. I have consented to this experiment, because I think that the Jarvises will come out of it harmless; and it is an understanding between me and Mr. Gage, that every sixpence they use generously and feelingly of the supposed fortune they will have, is to be made up to them as their own, when they shall find that I still live."

"Oh," said Mrs. Green, "I'm quite easy about what they will get, Mr. Bootle, so we won't argufy any more about it. You only agitate yourself about nothing; you know that is your way, and after all I think you were hasty."

"Hasty, hasty, Mrs. Green! hasty in what? In what was I hasty—tell me that."

"You were hasty in writing that cruel letter, which you wrote to your daughter—a letter which forbade her from ever offering to you an explanation of what seemed to be all so very wrong. You were hasty in that, Mr. Bootle; and you know that nobody is allowed to speak to you about it, and I suppose now I shall be discharged."

The old man's face betrayed the rush of powerful feelings that came over him. His lips moved, but he could not speak for some few moments; when, however, he did command his voice, sufficient to make himself heard, it was in a low, deep tone of much seriousness, that he said,—

"Once for all, once for all, I pray you to let it be understood between us, that you never revert to this subject. You know that, in consequence of your long and faithful services to me, I have so you a great respect. I am nearly desolate in the world as it is, do not make me altogether so, by forcing yourself away from me. Do not do that—no, no, no."

Mrs. Green began to be rather alarmed at the feelings she had awakened in the old man's breast, and to fear that she had, on the impulse of the moment, done more harm than good, in urging the point so far as she had. It was, therefore, in an apologetic tone that she replied to him,—

"Mr. Bootle, I did not intend to say what I have said,—the words slipped out unawares. You know I would not distress you; but you know well that I have strong feelings with regard to the subject we have been talking on, but I will say no more. I have only sincerely to hope that all will turn out well."

"Amen!" said the old man, "Amen! The whole affair agitates me, and I should not wonder, Mrs. Green, if it were to be the death of me; but if it is, what does it matter—what does it matter? The old, decayed trunk should give way to the vigorous young saplings that crowd around it to push it from the soil."

"There is no occasion, Mr. Bootle, for you to make any such remarks. We all know well enough how long creaking doors remain upon their hinges, and as for you're dying, that's neither here nor there; but I know what's put it into your head; it's making believe, and having an account of your death put in the London papers. I warrant if it had gone into the *County Chronicle*, there would have been many an inquiry."

"Well, well, say no more—say no more; we shall soon see what these Jarvises will do, and I think you will all find yourselves mistaken. My long acquaintance with Mr. Cage, and my great respect for you, Mrs. Green, induced me to consent; and now I'm going to take a little turn in the shrubbery, and will you be so good as to tell the young person you have to assist you in the kitchen to keep out of my way, for I don't want her to cross my path? she has not done so yet, and I don't want to begin."

"Oh, she don't want to come in your way, Mr. Bootle—not she; it's a likely thing, indeed, that she should be in the house a year and a-half, you seeing nothing of her, that all of a sudden she's to come across you now!"

" Well, well—well, well, say no more, Mrs. Green; I have placed myself at the disposal of yourself and Mr. Gage for a month, and I will not go back from my word, you may depend upon that. Give me my stick, Mrs. Green."

" And your gaiters?"

" No, Mrs. Green, not my gaiters. Do you take me for some old superannuated man, who can't move without his gaiters? No, thank God! I've got all my faculties about me yet, and you ought to know by this time that I never put on my gaiters if there's half a degree of temperature over sixty-five.'

The old man bustled from the breakfast-room to take his morning's walk in the extensive shrubberies connected with the Priory, and Mrs. Green, looking after him with an affectionate smile, muttered to herself,—

" Ah, you little know what other people are doing for you! You've got your own obstinacy all to blame: you won't listen to reason, and so you must be made to find out what's what, whether you like it or not. I always did hate those Jarvises I knew what they were from the very first. I understand such sort of people well. The wretches! But a day of reckoning will come for them, and they will soon be made to find out that honesty is—— There she is, as I'm a sinner! and if I don't run out and warn her she will run against the old man, for a certainty."

CHAPTER V.

THE INSTALMENT OF A FORTUNE.

LET us suppose that Mr. Bloomenback has dined with the Jarvises, and has freely partaken of all the good things of this life, which it suited the policy of that delightful family to lay before their legal adviser. A significant hint from Rhododenderon Jarvis had let Master Hannibal know that his company was not desirable, and that the attorney and his father chose to hold their conference without a spectator or an auditor.

This was a circumstance which did not give that young gentleman any great amount of trouble, for as from the first moment that he had become acquainted with his brilliant prospects to sink the dry-salting business, he rather enjoyed the liberty of going out and of running up a score, which he fully intended to do, at a neighbouring tavern.

Of course, a governor with fifteen thousand pounds a year would have been one of the most unreasonable persons on record to have had any objections to such a course; but whether he had or not certainly did not disturb Hannibal, who determined likewise, in his own expressive phraseology, to do the thing for the future uncommonly fast.

The conference between the two worthies, thus left alone, was long and confidential: to be sure, there was something in the shape of a little difference of opinion at one period, and that was when Bloomenback produced certain slips of paper with mysterious indentations at their corners, to signify that they represented stamps of a certain current denomination.

Mr. Rhododenderon Jarvis winced a little at the extent of these demands, but the lawyer conquered, and poured the oil of argument upon the stormy waves of contention.

In the course of half-an-hour he had the aforesaid stamps, duly filled up to the tune of ten thousand pounds, in his pocket-book, and then with smile he said,—

" I call that decidedly cheap. Nothing would be easier than to throw the whole affair into Chancery; you ought to know that, and, I dare say, do know it, as well as I. To be sure, Mr. Gage has told you that Mr. Brotherton is dead, but we don't know that for a certainty. An advertisement might produce him. The will of old Bootle, evidently made under a wrong impression, might be disputed on the ground that that was an insane impression."

" That will do—that will do: you have the stamps."

" True: but it's kind of me to make you so satisfied with what you've done, and you must bear in mind that even if you gained the cause, after, perhaps, eight or ten years of litigation, you not only lose all that time the enjoyment of a large property, but you come before the world with a damaged reputation."

" Pass the bottle—pass the bottle," said Jarvis: " do I not tell you that I am content? and you still think that I'm safe in taking the advance from Gage ?"

" Most unquestionably. Why should you not? He will require your note of hand for the amount; but what of that? you will only be charged legal interest for the amount in addition, probably, to a bonus, until you have the most ample funds at your disposal to meet the demand. We lawyers are tolerably careful, and don't lend our money for nothing. Take it, I say, take it, and I will be here to-morrow at the hour mentioned to meet Mr. Gage, for since my name has been used, I may as well appear in a *bona fide* manner as your legal adviser."

" Be it so—be it so; I am quite content that such should be the arrangement. It seems to me, Bloomenback, more like a dream than a reality, to think that I have jumped suddenly from an income of about seven hundred pounds per annum, achieved with toil and labour, to one of fifteen thousand pounds, which will give me no trouble."

" Yes; I must confess the success of the affair almost startles me, and but that Mr. Gage—a man who must be well informed upon the subject—is your informant, I should doubt the possibility of the fact. I wonder what steps are taken with regard to the old man's funeral. It perhaps would be as well if you were to go down to the Priory, and put on a decent show of grief for the occasion. I would accompany you, if you think it necessary, and we could make an inventory of the personal effects; possibly, there might be no objection to your taking possession at once, and residing there."

" No—no; I have heard the place spoken of; it is one of your old-fashioned, dismal-looking houses, with a hundred more rooms than any family could possibly want—one of those places that by their gloom are continually throwing you back upon your own thoughts; and—and as I have nothing very particular to think of that is remarkably pleasant, I prefer the life and animation of London. I want to see crowds about me—crowds half maddened with envy at my wealth and magnificence. What's the use of being a rich man, if it don't annoy everybody else?"

" That's a delightful truth," said Bloomenback; " there can be no doubt about it, and perhaps, after all, the shades and the seclusion of the Priory would not be just the things most likely to give you a comfortable opinion of yourself."

And so, in such amicable conversation, the sharp practitioner and his client sipped their port.

But we must not suppose that Mr. Jarvis or the great Hannibal were the only persons in the family who felt the change of fortune acutely, and although it is true that the magnitude of the amount which had been left to them was such that they scarcely had an appreciation of what it would produce, both Selina Jarvis and her mother had chalked out for themselves the path in life they meant to pursue; and with something of the same spirit that actuated Hannibal, Selina determined upon being a most decidedly fast young lady.

First and foremost, it was her resolution to astonish and excit the envy of all her female friends, and then to cut them in orde to aim at the establishment of connexions of a higher quality, for as she said to her mother, truly enough, " Folks may hate as much as they like, but as long as we've got the money, they'll come about us, and so soon as we convince them that we can do the thing properly, we shall have no want of great friends."

"That's uncommonly true, my dear," said Mrs. Jarvis, "and I certainly do rejoice at the whole affair, if it's only for the purpose of mortifying that odious Mrs. Smallbones, the draper's wife, who gives herself such airs and fancies. I should like, indeed, to give her a good splashing in the streets, with the wheels of our carriage. Only to think that, a week or two ago. I and your father were talking about the likelihoods of his becoming an alderman, and scarcely daring to think about the Lord Mayor's chair; but now, I suppose, we should hardly condescend to accept an invitation to the Mansion House."

"The Mansion House indeed!" said Selina, turning up her nose,—"St. James's will be the place for us."

"I say," said Job Brick, popping his head into the room; "there's Mr. Brown down stairs, shall I ask him up?"

"What, Brown, the hatter?"

"Yes," said Job, "and no mistake—the purveyor of four-and-nines; and precious brown they are, in a little while."

"Tell him," said Selina, "we are not at home."

"A lively thought, my dear," exclaimed her mother. "We must really, you know, learn to cut common people; and suppose, now, we should begin upon Brown, it would be a sort of practice, you know. Where is he, Job?"

"In the back-parlour," said Job; "he looks precious well-pleased, and he would have come up of his own accord for half a pin; you know his funny way, missus; he asked me how the cat and the kitten was—meaning you and Miss Selina."

"The what!" exclaimed Selina: "upon my word, the impertinence of common people in business is beyond everything; but we'll soon set Mr. Brown right."

Calling to their aid all the dignity that Bishopsgate could furnish, Mrs. Jarvis and her daughter sallied down stairs to extinguish Brown—who, with all the cool impertinence of an old friend of the family, had seated himself, with a very waggish air, upon a chair, on the back of which he leant his arms, as he exclaimed,—

"Come, come, ladies, this won't do. I'm quite sure there's something going on—quite positive, and to pretend to do without me is really quite an insult. I'll bet anybody a new hat you've had somebody to dinner."

" Sir, said Mrs. Jarvis, "our page, that is to say, one of our pages, informed us, you requested an interview about a—a—really I forget your name."

" Perhaps it's a mistake," said Selina; " he—he—he!"

For any indifferent spectator to have observed the countenance of Brown would have been a great physiognomical treat. We have heard of great geniuses finding their way from grave to gay, from lively to severe, but it was reserved for Mr. Brown to find his way at once from overbearing conceit and confidence to the very height of bewildered astonishment.

" What!—what!" he exclaimed; " don't you know me? Brown—you know Brown?"

" Do you know Brown?" said Selina to her mother, with the most *naive* air imaginable.

" Brown," said Mrs. Jarvis, looking up at the ceiling, as if she were in a brown study—"Brown—any relation to Smith?"

" Well! now, upon my life," said Brown, "it's very good—capital; oh! I see now what a goose I was; it's a joke—quite a joke. Ha! ha! devilish well done."

" My dear," said Mrs. Jarvis to her daughter, " I begin to think I do recollect something of a Mr. Brown, a dentist, that pulled your father's eye-tooth out; he can't possibly want us: it's a mistake—we beg to wish you a good morning, sir!'

" Good morning," said Selina; " we wish you an extremely good morning."

The ladies backed out of the room with what they considered wondrous grace, certainly leaving poor Brown in a state of bewilderment that baffles description.

His first movement was to walk up to the glass that was over the chimney-piece, and take a good look at himself; he then bestowed upon his ear a tolerable pinch, for the most serious doubts began to insinuate themselves to his mind, concerning his waking existence.

" I am Brown," he said, " John Brown, the hatter; oh yes,

c 3

there can be no mistake. I'm Brown—not know me! Mrs. Jarvis and Selina Jarvis not know me! Why—why, they dined at my house last Christmas-day. Not know me, indeed!—oh, it's a joke —a joke—it must be only a joke!—yet, how uncomfortable; really, I don't know what to think. Oh, you're here, are you?— Job, just look at me, that's a good fellow.'

"Ah," said Job, "I see you; they say as the great wonder is to see a dead donkey, there's lots of live ones."

"What do you mean, you scoundrel? what do you mean?"

"Oh, nothing particular."

"Job, now—come now, Job; do you see that?—there's a shilling, an easy earned shilling, Job; upon my life I don't get a shilling by many a hat I sell, and all I want you to do, my fine fellow, is just to tell me why they won't know me here now?"

"Thank ye," said Job; "haven't you heard?"

"Heard what—what?"

"Lord bless you! we have come into our property. I don't ow how many thousands a-week we've got now, but I think it's cout fifty-five. We don't know anybody now."

"The devil! you don't mean that, Job? I say, just tell me all bout it, from time to time, and I don't mind paying you. Who's tto 'em?"

"Old Bootle."

"What, the rich old Bootle left 'em his property? why, they say he had half a million of money. Oh, good gracious, and I might have married Selina Jarvis last year!"

"Well, you can have her now, you know: I don't want her."

"You, Job! who the deuce thought you did? I'll go home and write her a note: oh what a chance! It aint so much as fifty-five thousand a-week, Job, but it may be something devilish near that in a year for aught I know; and, I say, mum's the word, Job; don't say I asked you a question, and, if I marry Selina Jarvis, a twenty pound-note, Job, is yours."

"Something down," said Job, holding out his hand.

Mr. Brown winced at this, but, after a great deal of reluctance, he produced a sovereign, which he deposited in Job's rather dirty palm; and then he hurried home to indite the epistle which he hoped might yet have the effect of melting the heart of Selina Jarvis.

"What a go!" said Job; "it's an ill wind which blows nobody good. What a funny little note this is to me from Mr. Gage; let me see it again."

Job took from his pocket a crumpled piece of paper, and read, in a muttered voice,—

"Job Brick—It's quite by accident I found that you lived in the family of the Jarvises; you were an honest and a good lad when I knew you. Meet me to-night at my chambers in Lincoln's Inn at nine, for I've something particular to say to you."

"Very good," said Job, when he had finished this epistle, "of course I'll go; there's something queer, and loads of screws loose somewhere, I shouldn't wonder."

CHAPTER VI.

THE VISIT TO THE PRIORY.

When Mr. Bloomenback, late in the evening, left the house of the Jarvises, he walked with slow and steady steps, for he had not taken too much wine, to his chambers in New Inn; and there, by the very dim light of a small candle, he sat for an hour in deep thought.

Now and then he muttered to himself unconnected words and sentences; and then, just as the inn clock pealed forth the hour of eleven, for he had left early, he rose, and, with all the air of a man that had come to some fixed determination, he walked along with great rapidity towards Regent-street.

All persons who are acquainted with that locality are aware of the situation of Newman's posting-house, where, at any hour, a chaise and post-horses may be procured by those whom fortune has blessed with a sufficient amount of the circulating medium to enable them to avail themselves of that luxury.

The air and manner of Mr. Bloomenback were confident ; and, after a short interview with the proprietor of the establishment, during which Mr. Bloomenback produced a cheque-book and wrote a draft for the required amount, the ostlers were made to busy themselves in putting the horses to a chaise.

One of the post-boys in waiting was summoned to take his turn ; and, after mentioning to his companion that he had a long stage to go, but the gentleman promised to be liberal if the job was done fast, he mounted, and in two minutes more Mr. Bloomenback was rattling on towards Wiltshire.

No doubt the natural cunning and suspicion of the lawyer had induced this visit, which was intended for the Priory, in order to ascertain all particulars connected with the demise of Mr. Bootle.

We certainly have a sincere hope that the lawyer will be disappointed, and that he will find such preparations made as may delude him into the requisite belief ; but, whether or not, we have a sort of trusting confidence in Mr. Gage, who, no doubt, in some manner, will manage that the plot shall not fail in consequence of any artful dodge of Bloomenback's.

It was not a pleasant night to travel in ; and yet, strange to say, there were more travellers than one upon the road ; and scarcely had Bloomenback departed, when a gentleman strolled into Newman's yard, and requested a postchaise to be immediately procured, naming a place about ten miles off.

This was a matter easily arranged ; and, when the chaise was ready, the gentleman said a friend of his was waiting for him outside in Regent-street, which turned out to be the case, and the two together rattled off, surely by a coincidence merely, in the same direction as the chaise which had taken Bloomenback.

After getting clear of London, they stopped the post-boy, and one of them said to him,—

" Do you think that you could conveniently reach the next stage, by putting on extra speed, in a shorter space of time than the ten miles an hour we have specified for ?"

" No, sir," said the boy, " I don't think we could "—by-the-by, the boy was nearly fifty.

"But there are means of accelerating speed," said the stranger, as he produced a couple of sovereigns and placed them in the post-boy's hands.

"Ah! yes, sir," said the driver; "gentlemen as understands what business is can go at any pace they likes."

Another moment, and the pace, which had before been a short ten miles an hour, was quickened to something over twelve. The road was good, and, as it happened, hard and dry, so that by the time the inn was reached, at which a change of horses was to be procured in case the travellers wished to proceed further, Mr. Bloomenback had gained nothing by the start he had had, and the chaise in which he had departed from Regent-street was at the door, divested of the cattle that had drawn it so far.

The two strangers had not bargained to be carried beyond that spot: they were enveloped in ample cloaks, and they both dismounted from their vehicle, and, while Mr. Bloomenback remained shivering in the chaise, which he certainly had reasonable ground to suppose would convey him to the Priory in Wiltshire, these two mysterious strangers inquired for the post boy who had charge of his vehicle, and they soon got that individual into an adjoining room.

"Hark ye!" said one, "you look a well-meaning sort of fellow, and not like one who would do a bad action, even if he were well paid for it."

"Well, sir," said the post-boy, who had his own opinion that nothing very bad could come of this—"well, sir, all I can say is, that I suppose I'm no worse than other people."

"You're conveying a gentleman in your chaise to Wiltshire; he is not going upon the best of errands, and it can't matter much if he be delayed five or six hours on the road: now, I dare say, some ugly places are between here and the next two or three stages, accidents will happen, you know—there is a ten pound-note, and, as it will be a serious thing to you if you have an upset, in case such a thing should happen, you can keep it."

The post-boy placed his finger by the side of his nose, and gave it an extremely knowing perpendicular sort of movement.

"Lord bless you, sir!" he said, "I understand—a ten pound-note, did you say? Thank ye, sir. Now, I'll tell you just a wonderful thing; it has struck me all of a sudden that there's a nasty place called Datchley, about six miles on, and I never felt so sure of anything in all my life as that the blessed post-chaise I shall be a driving of will upset just by that very place. It's a most remarkable thing, do you know, sir; but, about a fortnight ago, I was a driving of an old gentleman along the North-road, and a young gentleman he says to me afore I starts, 'Bob,' says he, 'you'll upset that old gentleman as sure as fate.' 'No,' says I, 'I won't.' 'Yes,' says he, 'you will; and, as that'll do you no good in your perfession,' says he, 'mind ye, if you do upset him, call upon me for a five pound-note;' and, would you believe it, sir, I did upset him?"

"Am I to be kept here all night?" said the voice of Mr. Bloomenback from the chaise window. "The horses are put to; you rascal! why do you not go on?"

"Don't ye hear him; he's getting impatient for his spill—he's a rum un, I can see that. Ah! it is a melancholy thing; but we shall have a downer at Datchley."

"You see, Henry," said one of the gentlemen to the other, when they were alone; "you see, Henry, that money is all powerful for good or for evil."

"It is indeed, sir."

"Well, well, at all events our friend Bloomenback will not reach the Priory sufficiently soon to take its inhabitants off their guard; you will, no doubt, find it quite easy to get a horse here; ride on, and let every preparation be made to meet Bloomenback, and remember that, possibly, upon the exertions you make, depend the cause of innocence and virtue."

"Trust me, sir; nothing shall be wanting upon my part, for the sake of one who, you know, is so dear to me that her slightest wish becomes a law; you know that I would take a thousand times more trouble than this enterprise gives me."

"I know it—I know it! Go then at once, Henry, and Heaven speed you! It was well, indeed, that we kept such an accurate watch upon Bloomenback, or the rascal would certainly have outwitted us."

" Yes; and yet one would hardly have supposed he could have had any suspicion."

" I scarcely think it a suspicion; but, you know, to be cautious, and to guard against even any possibility of a mistake, is part of his profession—moreover, probably, a little cupidity may have a share in the business. He has an eye possibly to the personal effects of Mr. Bootle. Hark! The chaise is starting. Lose no time now, but ride on, and I will return to town."

The inquiry for a saddle-horse was at once answered in the affirmative, and the young man, who was called Henry by his elder companion, was soon upon the road, following rapidly in the track of the post-chaise which conveyed Mr. Bloomenback upon his expedition.

The senior—whom probably our readers may suspect to be no other than Mr. Gage—proceeded to town again with fresh horses, having thus despatched a distant relative to whom he was warmly attached, and who was articled to him, in pursuit of the wily professional gentleman from New Inn.

As Mr. Bloomenback rattled along in his chaise, he became conscious that now and then there was a slight dash of rain against the windows, and that the night was getting stormy and uncomfortable. He heard a clock strike two, and he shuddered at the thought that he had before him a number of hours of positive discomfort to wade through; but still he had an object, and as that, like most of his objects, was one of a pounds, shillings, and pence character, it went very far towards reconciling him to the disposition of affairs.

But the road grew darker and darker; and although he carefully wiped the vapour from off the inside of the glasses, and strove to look out into the night, he could not see an inch beyond him.

All was blackness and obscurity—a blackness that looked as if it could have been felt; and every now and then, when he did fancy he was beginning to see a little, there came such a dash of cold rain against the window of the carriage, that he involuntarily drew back into its furthest corner, and told himself how very prudent and pleasant it would be to have a nap.

But the howling of the wind without, and every now and then a tremendous jerk of the vehicle as it fell into a rut of the road, prevented the possibility of anything in the shape of repose.

With his teeth clenched, therefore, through which, now and then, he muttered curses, Mr. Bloomenback was compelled to endure the miseries of certainly a rougher road than he thought the whole country of England could have furnished.

"Confound the fellow," he muttered; "where can he be driving me to? Hilloa! postilion, stop! stop! Where are you going, you rascal? This is not a high road, I know."

"What did you say, sir?" said the postilion, drawing up. "What did you say about your eye, sir?"

"I say this is not a high road. Where are you taking me to?"

"Oh! no, sir, it is not a high road—it's a cross-way we always take to Datchley, and it saves a matter of a mile and a half at least."

"At the expense of dislocating every bone in my skin. Get out of it as quickly as you can, or we shall be upset, to a certainty."

"Very good, sir; you shall have it all your own way."

Away rattled the chaise quicker than before. Mr. Bloomenback felt it rocking from side to side. He clutched nervously at the lining to keep his equilibrium; then there came a fearful lurch, and the vehicle ran upon two wheels for a few yards. A shriek burst from Bloomenback, and then, with a fearful crash, over went the chaise.

———

CHAPTER VII.

THE HORSEMAN.

SUCH men as Mr. Bloomenback are not generally among the most courageous of the great human family, and when that specimen of legal profundity found himself going over in the chaise, the cry that burst from his lips was one that would almost have melted the pump of New Inn to tears, albeit it had no such effect upon the flinty heart of the post-boy, who, being quite prepared for the upset, came to no damage.

"Woa! woa!" he cried; "woa, cattle, will you, now?"

"Murder! murder!" shouted Mr. Bloomenback. "Murder! Help—oh, help!"

"Why, what the deuce," cried the post-boy, "need you make such a disturbance, sir,—you can't be much hurt, or you'd not be able to make so much noise about it? Any limbs broken?"

"Oh, I don't know; I am smashed, I think, and dreadfully shaken. let me out! Oh, you scoundrel, you were recommended to me as such a steady driver, and now, you villain, you have nearly broken my back. But I'll bring my action—yes, I shall have famous grounds for an action, and, as sure as I'm a professional man, I'll bring an action for breach of contract and special damages."

"What! are you a lawyer?"

"Let me out—let me out, I say, I want to get out—never you mind what I am—it's no business of yours—let me out, I say!"

"O dear no! If I'd have knowed you was a lawyer at first, you wouldn't a got me to drive you. I never knowed but one lawyer, and he was the ruin of me as safe as bricks, he was. A lawyer are you?"

During this time, Mr. Bloomenback was certainly not in the most comfortable predicament in the world, for the chaise had been turned over completely on one side, and he had got jammed in across it in such a manner that he could not move. Certainly, if the post-boy had wished to do so, he might have opened the upper door, and let him out, or rather dragged him out; for Mr. Bloomenback was himself quite helpless, but *that* the elderly boy was in no haste to do, and now, as he listened, he heard the regular tramp of horse's feet approaching.

Guessing that this was one of the parties, who, from some cause unknown to him, was intent upon stopping the progress of the lawyer, he thought it would be as well to temporise with him until the horseman came up, so he said,—

"Well, well! though you is a lawyer, I don't want to keep you in the chaise no longer nor I can help, so give us hold of your hand, and I will pull you out."

By laying hold of the hand of Mr. Bloomenback, and giving him a hearty pull, the post-boy got him out of the chaise, but it was into the dirt he got him; for the road at that point was by no means in the pleasantest state or most salubrious condition, and the attorney got well soused in some most objectionable mire.

By this time the horseman had reached the spot, and drawing rein, he cried out loudly,—

"What's this, eh? who stops the road?"

"Oh, it's only a little spill, sir," said the post-boy—"the chaise upset, that's all, and there it must lay, for two people aint enough to get it right again, though I don't think anything is broken but the windows."

"Sir," said Mr. Bloomenback, in an imploring tone, "will you, in this emergency, lend a helping hand? I have a long journey before me, and it is a great object to me to be able to perform it quickly. This rascal of a post-boy, through his own carelessness, has upset the chaise; but I think that, by your assistance, we may have it up again, as I see he has freed the horses from it."

"I beg to decline," said the horseman; "I have no time to lose; I am going down to Wilts, and my mission is an urgent one."

"To Wilts!" exclaimed Mr. Bloomenback; "why, I was going there, to Mr. Bootle's, at the Priory."

"Mr. Who?"

"Bootle. The rich Mr. Bootle. If you know anything of Wilts, you have heard of him."

"I have heard of him, indeed; and if you are upset on your journey to Mr. Bootle's, it's quite providential, and you may spare yourself any more trouble, for I can tell you he is dead. You need go no further."

There was a pause of a moment's duration or so, and then Bloomenback said, with an air of suspicion.—

"But, sir, although you tell me that Mr. Bootle is dead, and that, consequently, it is of no use my going to him, how comes it that you don't likewise feel the inutility of continuing your journey?"

"Oh! I'm going to him because he is dead. If you were to tell me he was alive, I should turn my horse's head to town again. My name is Finch. I am Finch the—I think I may take upon myself, although I am speaking of myself, to say—great undertaker. It's rather muggy weather, and the old man don't keep very well, so our agent in Wilts has written to say that a leaden coffin is necessary at once, and I am going down myself to see him comfortably packed in it."

"You—you are quite sure. There is no mistake?"

"Mistake about what?"

"Well, well! Nothing, nothing! Let it pass. I—I certainly, being assured that Mr. Bootle is no more, can do no good by calling upon him in Wilts. 'Tis true I have paid my money for the whole journey, but better lose that than my time likewise. Yes, I will go to town again—I will go to town at once."

"As you please," said the horseman; it makes no difference to me. Good night! I'm sorry I can't lend you a helping hand but I'm really in a hurry."

He trotted off, and the sound of his horse's feet soon died away in the distance."

"Hark you," said Bloomenback to the post-boy, " I have now got information enough to warrant me in going back again. Go and try to get assistance to raise the chaise, and I will say nothing of the upset, since it has spared me so long and useless a journey."

"Ah! now, that's what I call coming to reason," said the post-boy; "I can see a light—most likely from the window of a far a-house; and if you wait here, and give a shout if you see anything coming, so that they might not tumble over the chaise, I will get back again as soon as ever I can."

This guardianship of the road was accepted by Mr. Bloomenback, who was certainly very much shaken by his fall, and as he paced to and fro to endeavour to get himself rid of the trembling nervousness that had come over him, he muttered to himself,—

"Surely, there can be no doubt now. This is confirmation strong. I cannot now have any suspicions; and, after all, I do not now regret the adventures of the last hour, since they have sufficed to give me the strongest possible circumstantial evidence of the death of Bootle, of which before I don't know that I ought to have had any doubts about, and yet, somehow, I feel very much inclined to make assurance doubly sure. Oh! of course, he is dead now. Ha! ha! Folks are not usually put into leaden coffins unless they have shuffled off their mortal coils. No, no! He is dead, sure enough, and my mind may now be at ease."

As the post-boy had either conjectured, or knew from having travelled the same road before, the light he saw did proceed from the windows of a farm-house, at which he procured three or four labourers, whose strength was fully sufficient to right the post-chaise, which had, as has been remarked, sustained no damage beyond the smashing of the window on the side which had fallen next to the ground.

Of course the post-boy had chosen the spot of the disaster, if disaster it might be called, well, and had taken care that in accomplishing the upset of the lawyer, he did as little damage to his master's property as possible, for that he knew he would be held responsible for, but he could very well afford to pay for a new pane of plate-glass out of the amount he had received from Mr. Gage for committing the feat of cunning—the chance of doing Bloomenback some grievous bodily harm.

It was not a little provoking, however, to the man of law, when he found he was asked to pay for the pleasure of having been upset, which he was, for the post-boy would not plead guilty to having a sixpence, and it was not likely that the man who came from the farm house would exactly feel inclined to work for the mere love of the thing.

Half a sovereign was therefore most unwillingly disbursed by Bloomenback, who, being then assured that the chaise was all right, and that the only inconvenience he was likely to feel would proceed from the cold night air coming in through the broken window, gave orders to get towards London again.

And yet, such was the kind of dread of being taken in that came over Bloomenback, that no sooner did he find himself getting along towards the metropolis again, at the rate of ten miles an hour, than he began to regret that he had turned back; but he reasoned himself out of that feeling. The leaden coffin did the business completely.

"Oh yes, it's all right," he muttered; "of course old Bootle is dead; a corpse is not altogether such a pleasant sight, that I need be anxious to travel so many miles just for the pleasure of looking at it. I am quite content. The leaden coffin is the thing, oh, that is most convincing; and, after all, it was devilish lucky I met with Finch, the undertaker. By-the-by, I might as well have asked him where he lived; I will look in the Directory for his name when I get home."

Mr. Bloomenback felt some little difficulty about how he was to account for his great inconsistency of conduct to the Jarvises. The fact is, he had certainly not told Jarvis that he intended to go to Wilts; it was quite an after determination, although not an after thought, when he had reached his chambers.

He had, indeed, as we are aware, promised to be at the Jarvises on the morrow, when Mr. Gage had agreed to make his second visit; and he had slipped a letter into a post-office that was open all night, before he got the chaise from Newman's, stating to Rhododenderon Jarvis that he could not keep his appointment; for it might be a day or two before he concluded some business that suddenly called him from town.

Now, however, he could make his appearance and meet Mr. Gage, so that it might have the appearance to his good friend Jarvis, as if he were playing some tricks with him.

"But that can't be helped," thought the attorney. "He must just think what he likes, and say what he likes. One comfort is, that he is quite helpless, and that I have got his promissory notes for ten thousand pounds. Ha! ha! ha! ten thousand pounds!—I will have more than that. Do you think that I am going to let you, Mr. Jarvis, off for ten thousand pounds? No, no, not at all; I have been instrumental in getting you the large fortune you will possess, and I do not see at all why we should not share and share alike."

With these comfortable reflections, Mr. Bloomenback proceeded towards town again, and had he not been so buried in one corner of the post-chaise, and so engaged in his own reflections, he might, in the dim grey light of early morning, have seen a horseman dash past him likewise on the road to London at a hard gallop, and he might, from the *contour* of the figure, and the general appearance, have suspected him to be no other than Mr. Finch.

The fact is, that the young man who had been deputed to ride to the Priory by Mr. Gage, when he saw that by an accident he had fully succeeded in turning aside from his purpose Bloomenback, used his own discretion, and came back again; for as the lawyer from the New Inn did not choose to continue his journey to Wilts, there certainly was no occasion for the student from Lincoln's Inn to do so.

Verily, if it were once for the first time in his life, Mr. Bloomenback was, most certainly, terribly outwitted upon this occasion.

Fatigued, exhausted, hungry, and half dead from the fall, as well as from the jolting he got in the post-chaise over so many miles of country, Mr. Bloomenback reached his chambers in New Inn between seven and eight in the morning, and found it absolutely necessary at once to seek some repose. He had an alarum clock, and that he set to eleven, so that he would have some hours' rest, and yet be in time to get to the Jarvises by about the hour that Mr. Gage might be expected to make his second visit, on which interesting occasion it was hoped that he would not go back from his word as regarded the advance of the five thousand pounds.

At nine o'clock on the preceding evening, Job Brick had, according to appointment, made his way to Lincoln's Inn, and had been duly closeted with Mr. Gage for about half an hour.

What it was Job was required to do, will best appear as he does it—suffice it for the present, that as he left the chambers, he turned to Mr. Gage, and said,—

" You may depend upon me, sir. They dussn't turn me away. I know too much of all their secrets; and bless her heart, Miss Marianna shall want for nothing, you may depend, sir. I'll take care of her ; and besides, let you know, sir, all as happens. They shan't so much as move one of their little fingers, but I'll take notice of it. Lor! I never heard such a rummy go as it all is in all my life. I'm much obliged to you, sir—and feels as happy as a king, I does. Good night to you, sir! and you may depend upon seeing me on Wednesday.

" That will do, Job; good night!"

CHAPTER VIII.

THE MEMORANDUM.

DID any of the Jarvises sleep that night? Did they, after the usual snarling evenings they spent together upon ordinary occasions, retire to repose with all the calmness of domestic comfort— for there was certainly no great amount of affection among them ? Oh no. The visions of their wealth seemed to grow upon them hour by hour, and there was not one of them but who tossed about that live-long night, conning over schemes of ambition for the future.

Miss Selina and her mother had made a goodly common on the manner in which they had treated the aspiring Mr. Brown, and Hannibal had been, as he said, " going it rather fast" all the evening, and had come home with a dim perception that he had indulged himself certainly with *good cœur suff*.

He did manage to get to bed in his boots; but then he had

heard of other great geniuses doing so before his time, and although the bedstead, somehow or another, after he was laying down, had a propensity to spin round and round, he felt tolerably happy and comfortable.

The repentance was to come. Wait a bit, Master Hannibal, and you will discover that " going it fast " has its accompanying disagreeables, and that, somehow or another, people's heads will ache, even if they be heirs in expectancy of fifteen thousand per annum.

As for Jarvis himself, his dreams of arrogance were fully sufficient to disturb him. The only trouble he found was what to do first, by way of showing to the world that he could do anything he pleased ; but every now and then the thought of the young child Marianna came across him with a disagreeable twinge.

He very much wished that she would be so kind as to die. He had never seen her, and he wondered if she were consumptive. He remembered hearing it said that her mother had been so, and he knew that consumption was a nice hereditary sort of disorder— she might die; but then again there was no certainty, and she might live to be a perpetual reproach to him if he were niggardly towards her, and a perpetual source of deep regret if he were otherwise.

As for the extravagant proposition of Mr. Gage, that he should settle ten thousand pounds upon her—he could not think of such a thing—it was by far too preposterous ; and yet what excuse could he make for not doing something handsome, while to do something that merited that expression would have driven his selfish soul almost mad.

Full of these reflections, the possessor—as he believed himself to be—of half a million of money, fell asleep at last, after being far more distracted in his mind about ten thousand pounds that he was asked to do an act of common justice with, than he was delighted with the acquisition of fifty times that amount.

Selfish, grovelling fool! is it for such as thou art that the bright glittering gold has been dug from the deep mine to dazzle the eyes of humanity? Oh! how grievously little must old Mr.

Bootle have known of the great world, when he mistook such a man as you are for a kind and liberal spirit! How very necessary did it become that, by some practical means, the rich old man, who felt he had so much cause to mourn, should be undeceived; and, in that process of unmasking Jarvis, let us hope that the innocent and the beautiful will achieve a glorious triumph. They must—they shall!

*   *   *   *   *

When the Jarvises assembled in their breakfast-room on the following morning, the events of the preceding day seemed to be almost of a dreamy character; and it was only by question and answer among themselves, that they became convinced that it was, indeed, real. They were all there but Hannibal.

Alas! fast-going Hannibal! He was reaping the bitter fruits of attempting to effect in his stomach an amalgamation of bottled stout, port wine, champagne, devilled kidneys, and Burton ale. How devoutly he wished himself dead when he awoke in the morning, and found himself condemned to all the horrors of a sick headache! With what tottering feet and what abject groans he made his way to the water-bottle on his toilette-table, with the hope that a draught from it would, in some measure, allay the pangs he suffered!

Oh! fallacious expectation! The cold stream, as it trickled down his throat, gave but a momentary relief to thirst, and none at all to the throbbing headache, that seemed to him as if a dozen tinkers were at work in his brain, hammering it up into lumps, beating it out again, and making such rude riot

"Within the chambers of the soul,"

that the disheartened, agonised, fast young gent would have given a bill, ante-dated, for a cool thousand, but for five minutes' ease from his sufferings. But, then, if people will go fast, they must take the consequences.

An inquiry from his father concerning his absence from the breakfast-table elicited a report from Job Brick, to the effect that he thought Mr. Hannibal had a pain in his great toe.

D

Mr. Jarvis rather guessed the real state of the case, and said no more. He did not particularly care whether Hannibal came down or not, and, perhaps, he thought, that it was not a *very* bad thing for him to have such a warning—that to go so very fast was not exactly the way to ensure a large amount of gratification.

During the morning's repast, a note, highly perfumed, was handed to Miss Selina, which she opened with a listless air. It came from Brown, the hatter, and contained an ardent avowal of attachment, and an offer of his hand, his heart, and all his hats; but it did not kindle in the breast of the young lady the least amount of kindred emotion, and, without a remark, the note was tossed into her mother's lap.

When Mrs. Jarvis had read it, she exclaimed,—

"Well, really, the impertinence of common people in business is dreadful!"

"Shocking!" said Selina.

"What's the matter now?" asked Mr. Jarvis, as he glanced up from the newspaper he was trying to read, although he was by far too busy in his own thoughts really to understand what the precise words were that met his eyes. "What's the matter now?"

"Oh! only an offer," said Mrs. Jarvis, "from Brown to Selina."

"Indeed! He is too late. Poor Brown—he is too late!"

"Too late, indeed!" said Selina; "I'm sure I never meant to stoop to pick up nothing. I don't know what you mean about too late."

"Well, well, it's no matter; we need not quarrel about that; but you can send him an answer, telling him that you are so surprised at his presumption, that you must request he will not again favour the house with a visit. The sooner we can get rid of the City connexions, the better."

"Oh, of course, when we have shown them what we are."

"I will manage that, by securing invitations to the next entertainment of the Lord Mayor, and then we will come into the City in a manner that I rather think will make some people open their eyes."

"I believe you, we will; oh! won't it be capital, ma?"

"My dear, it will be capital; and I only hope that the odious Mrs. Smallbones will be at her window, and see us dash along in our barouche. I know it will nearly be the death of her, and I certainly should like to make that woman seriously ill."

Mr. Jarvis resumed his newspaper, and when the time approached at which he expected the appearance of Mr. Gage, he got so very nervous and fidgetty that he was forced to lay it down again.

Now, Mr. Jarvis was tolerably well to do, and he could have extracted enough money from his own resources at once, if he had pleased, in order to make a dash, but the getting £5,000 from Mr. Gage had been made such an important item by Bloomenback, as a proof of the *bona fide* nature of the whole transaction, that Mr. Jarvis now waited, with no small amount of impatience, for the consummation of that part of the business.

He had duly received the note from Bloomenback, advising him that that gentleman would not be able to show himself in the morning, and he was rather surprised, but not afflicted; for the exorbitant demands of Bloomenback were of such a character, that he dreaded now his coming into the place.

We happen to know, however, that the attorney will be there, despite his note to the contrary, and at half-past eleven, when Job Brick came to announce, as Jarvis thought, Mr. Gage, he was disappointed to hear the name of Bloomenback come from his lips, and in another moment that individual himself made his appearance.

"You surprise me," said Jarvis. "I had a note from you, saying that legal business, some short distance from town, prevented you coming."

"Yes," said Bloomenback, "but I have, by great trouble, succeeded in putting it off; considering, as I do, that your affairs are the most important matters I have in hand now."

"Oh! you are very good."

"Mr. Gage," announced Job Brick.

"Ah! he is punctual," muttered Bloomenback: "a good sign. Introduce me at once, Jarvis."

Mr. Jarvis did the amiable, and duly introduced the two professional gentlemen to each other. The introduction, on the part of Mr. Gage, was not attended with any extraordinary amount of excitement or gratification. He only inclined his head slightly, and then, turning to Mr. Jarvis, he said,—

"Sir, a rather singular circumstance has occurred, in the shape of a memorandum, I found among some papers of the late Mr. Bootle, that I happen to have by me."

The countenance of Bloomenback fell, and Mr. Jarvis shook so that he was forced to totter into a seat, for he dreaded that the little memorandum might, by some possibility, make a difference in the disposition of Mr. Bootle's property, and that all his visions of future greatness might be about to vanish in the dim halo of a chancery suit.

"Do not be alarmed, gentlemen," said Mr. Gage, "the memorandum in no way affects the disposition of Mr. Bootle's property."

Jarvis and Bloomenback breathed again.

"No, gentlemen," added Mr. Gage, ' it merely says, that believing, as the late Mr. Bootle did, that the family circle of the Jarvises was quite irreproachable, and a pattern of calm domestic happiness, he desires that on his death Marianna Brotherton may become a member of that circle. I was surprised to find the memorandum, but it is most undoubtedly in the handwriting of the late Mr. Bootle, and is, I really think, the only one instance in which he has written the name of his grandchild. What do you say to it, Mr. Jarvis?"

"Oh! I—I don't object,—oh no, of course."

"The memorandum then goes on further to say, that Mrs. Shuter, a great aunt of his, Mr. Bootle's, will call occasionally and see the child, giving it moral advice,; and I can only say that, for an old lady, you will find Mrs. Shuter quite a sensible person, and one you will like very much; and if you fancy her now and then a tax upon your patience, you will, I am sure, put up with it."

———

CHAPTER IX.

THE ARRIVAL.

IT cannot be said that either of these occurrences were of a very pleasing character to Mr. Jarvis, and yet they were of a nature which he could not, under the circumstances, very well object to. Mr. Bloomenback, too, fidgetted a little over the affairs, but then he was so very sure old Bootle was dead. He thought again of Mr. Finch and the leaden coffin.

"I don't see, Mr. Jarvis," he said, "that you can have any objection to the residence of Miss Marianna in your very excellent family, and as for the visits of the old lady mentioned by Mr. Gage, they cannot, you know, last for ever!"

"Certainly not," said Gage, "she is eighty something already."

"Well then, let it be so," said Jarvis; "and now, Mr. Gage, you were kind enough to say yesterday that you did not object to an advance, in the shape of a few thousands."

"Nor do I, sir, now; but, of course, with us men of the law, business is business, you know, and we are forced to be cautious; I shall require a promissory note from you on demand, and another name at the back."

"Indeed!"

"Yes, that's the only way in which I can do the business; I ask for no tangible security, because I myself drew the will of the late Mr. Bootle. I have no objection to your name, you see, but things must be regular; and as I make no secret to you, it is not my own money, but the money of a client, that I will advance; I must have two names to show him, besides my own."

"Oh, you will endorse likewise," said Bloomenback.

"I must."

"Then I have no objection to back the note, under such circumstances; of course it's all right. I must, as you say, be paid as soon as Mr. Jarvis is put in possession of his property."

"Exactly: if you have a stamp, I will give you a cheque at once for the amount of £4,800, which will be considered as £5,000, if you please, reckoning interest and procuration fee, which you know is quite regular, Mr. Bloomenback."

"Oh, yes, yes."

"I have written to the gentleman, Mr. Smith, who has the will, to come back as soon as he can, and at all events to communicate with me immediately, stating that he is ready to produce such a will, and the moment I get his letter I shall place it in your hands."

"Oh, that's all right," said Bloomenback, as Jarvis glanced at him, as if for advice; "that's all right enough; it's quite regular all that, of course."

The promissory note was duly drawn, and with a calmness that was delightful to see, Mr. Gage wrote a cheque for £4,800, which he handed to Mr. Jarvis, saying,—

"This, sir, is the first instalment of one of the most brilliant fortunes it ever fell to the lot of a private individual to hold in this country. This mere bagatelle you can look upon just as a sort of earnest of what is yet to come, and now I can tell you, that anticipating your reply about Marianna Brotherton, she will be here in the course of the day, by my orders; you will find her a young and amiable girl, and I do hope that she will be happy with you."

"To-day!" said Jarvis. "Quick work!"

"Yes, but the poor child was at school; and as the death of Mr. Bootle may produce much public talk about him and his affairs, I thought it might spare Marianna much annoyance, if she were removed at once to your paternal care, and I doubt not but you will behave liberally towards her, as she is wholly and entirely dependent upon you."

"Oh! of course," said Mr. Jarvis; "although it is not pleasant to have strangers and interlopers in one's house, I don't wish to stand in the way of any wish of Mr. Bootle's. It's not exactly to be expected that we should feel precisely towards such an individual, base-born as she is, as we should feel towards a more respectable sort of individual."

"But you will be pleased to recollect always," remarked Mr. Gage, very mildly, "that her being base-born is not exactly her fault."

" No, no, I don't say it is; but we have our feelings upon those subjects."

" Which, I am sure, do you infinite honour. And now, sir, as I presume we have concluded all the business we can, at the present time, satisfactorily get through, I will take my leave of you, merely saying that, in the course of the day, Miss Marianna Brotherton will arrive, accompanied by one trunk, from her school."

With these words Mr. Gage made his bow and his exit, leaving Jarvis and Cousin Bloomenback sufficiently dazzled by the **five** thousand pounds in hand, not to care very much for the accession to the family arrangements in the shape of a young girl who was hourly expected.

" Hark ye !" said Bloomenback; " as a matter of the most ordinary discretion, it will be desirable for you to behave well to this child. You know as well as I what she really is."

" I have no fear of her; old Bootle is dead, and I don't see what can happen wrong. As for her staying with me, it shall all depend upon circumstances, and I don't see why she shouldn't be put away to some cheap place, where she will not be an annoyance to anybody."

" I say," said Job Brick, popping in his head, " here's a hackney coach come, and a little girl."

" 'Tis she, indeed," said Jarvis; " truly this Mr. Gage has made quick work of it."

" Have her shown up here at once," said Bloomenback, " and you will soon discover whether she is likely or not to be a dangerous customer."

Mr. Jarvis shook a little at the idea of facing that young girl, whom he knew he had so deeply injured, and towards whom his selfish nature would not permit him to act even with a discreet liberality which would have saved him from a breath of reproach. He paced the room anxiously after having given orders for her to be shown up, and played nervously with the guard-chain of his watch, while Mr. Bloomenback assumed a favourite attitude of his, which consisted of having his back to a window, so that his whole face was obscured in shadow, and any one advancing to speak to him had the advantage or disadvantage, as it might be, of the light full upon their countenance.

Job Brick flung the door open, and Marianna Brotherton, with a timid step, advanced into the apartment.

She was but a child, for she had not reached her tenth year; but she was so tall for her age that she might have passed for a girl of twelve or thirteen. Her hair was of the glossiest black that could be conceived, and, as Jarvis saw at a glance, she inherited a pair of large, earnest-looking eyes, such as were a peculiar feature in her poor mother's face; yet, young as this girl was, Jarvis and the attorney both felt that Nature had done much for her in giving her something of a commanding expression about her air and general features—it must have been so, or why did they both shrink, bold-faced, worldly men as they were, from one so very young in years, and who could have so little power to harm them?

The pause that ensued was an awkward one, and Jarvis, who was now more nervous, and, therefore, could less endure it, than Bloomenback, broke it by saying,—

"You—you are Marianna Brotherton, are you not?"

"That is my name," was the girl's reply; and the deep cadence of her melancholy voice seemed to speak as if she had already suffered some oppression. She might have been taunted with her peculiarity of position—the mother's presumed error may have been used as a means of reproach against the child—there are people who are capable of even such iniquity as that—and hence, perhaps, the dawn of her young life may have been clouded by harshness.

"Well, well," said Jarvis, "I suppose you understand you are to remain here; and, if you make yourself agreeable, and give us no trouble, we shall have no objection."

"None whatever," said Bloomenback; "but you had better understand, my girl, at once, that the less you say about who you are the better."

"I have been told," said the child, "that I am poor and destitute; there never was but one person who spoke a kindly word to me."

" Indeed ! and who was that ?"

" A Mrs. Shuter, who came once to see me at my school—she is so very old that I could scarcely hear her speak ; and she wep' too, so much, that it was very sad to hear her."

" Indeed !" said Bloomenback ; " perhaps you expect to se her again ?"

" I do—I hope and expect to see her again. You do not know how a heart like mine treasures up even a small kindness. I am not so very used to caresses as all that."

" This Mrs. Shuter," whispered Jarvis to Bloomenback, " will troublesome to us, I feel convinced she will, and something must be done to put a stop to her visits."

" Say nothing of it at present ; it may be necessary to endure them for a while. Say not a word—say not a word, but give general orders that this young girl is to be seen to. I do not mean to tell you that you will have her long as an inmate of your house ; but, at present, it is absolutely necessary that she should be such. For a time the eyes of the world will be bent upon you, and your conduct will be accurately scrutinised ; but, when the nine days' wonder of your new fortunes has passed away, you can do as you please. Send for your wife or daughter, and give this child in charge to them."

" I will—I will. Do you not see with what a strange expression—something I think there is of suspicion in it—she regard; me ? Do you not perceive that such is the case ? I shall not be able to endure for long her presence."

" You need not endure it—let it rest—she need never en counter you—you are well aware of that. In a large establishment, such as you can be the master of, a dozen persons may be under the same roof, and you know nothing of it."

" It must be so, if she remains with me. Ring, Bloomenback ; you are next to the bell."

Bloomenback did so ; and when Job Brick, who seemed to be in very close proximity to the door, answered the summons, Mr. Jarvis said to him,—

"Take this young lady, Job, and show her to your mistress; say that it is Miss Brotherton."

The child looked at Job with a dubious expression of countenance, and, doubtless, the look that he put on was fully intended to assure her of the most friendly state of feeling; only, as it consisted of a series of nods and winks such as she certainly had never seen before, it was not very likely that she could draw a correct conclusion from Job's ballet performances. She followed him, however, from the room; and then, after a short whispered conference together of about a quarter of an hour's duration, Jarvis and Bloomenback separated, but the latter took the cheque with him, promising, within an hour, to send the lion's share to the drysalter.

"I say," said Job to Marianna, when they were outside the door of the apartment, "I say, don't you be afraid of anybody here; I'll be down upon them if they should say half a word to you that you don't like, and mind, I'm to be your friend under all circumstances. I'm going to stick to you like a brick, and it won't last long, you know, that is to say, you don't know that, but I can tell you it won't; I mustn't tell you too much though, because I promised I wouldn't."

"Much about what?" said the girl. "I was happy and contented enough where I was; why am I moved away, and brought among people, who, I can perceive, do not love me, and who have already said enough to convince me that they look upon me as an encumbrance."

"There," said Job, looking around him, as if appealing to some invisible geni, "there, I told ye so; I knew she'd ask me all sorts of questions that I daren't answer, and here I am in that uncomfortable fix: now I tell you what it is, Miss Marianna, I know a good deal that I mustn't tell you; but I will tell you this much—you needn't care nothing for nobody, and you needn't mind what they say to you; all you've got to do is not to forget it, because you'll be asked about it some of these days, and it won't look the thing then not to know."

The girl looked astonished, as well she might, in finding she had so strange a friend, who, although she had never seen him before, evidently seemed fully prepared, from some previous knowledge of her, to take her part, and do her all the benefit in his power.

"We mustn't stand talking here," said Job, "or else they'll suspect us, and I might have to leave, whether I like it or not; so come on, and I'll take you to the cat and the kitten, as Mr. Brown calls them, though, Lord bless you! the kitten is getting rather a respectable old mouser; but don't you mind a pin what they say to you—they won't make the most pleasant remarks in the world; but if you go on perpetually never-minding, where's the odds?"

With this highly philosophical admonition, Job led Marianna to an apartment, where he knew that the mother and daughter were in close conversation, and, flinging open the door without any abundance of ceremony, he exclaimed,—"Miss Marianna Brotherton!"

There was quite a faint shriek from Selina, and Mrs. Jarvis immediately put on a look of frozen dignity.

"She is to stay here," added Job Brick, "and you're to do the best you can for her, all of you;" and then with another series of winks at Marianna, to signify that she was to be afraid of nothing, and that, let Miss Selina or Mrs. Jarvis put on their most awful frowns, she, Marianna, might laugh thereat, he left the room; but scarcely had he done so, when Mr. Jarvis walked in; and, beckoning his wife and daughter up to a window, he spoke to them earnestly for some few seconds; and it was evident, from the glance they all cast upon Marianna, that she was the object of their discourse. Without, then, taking any notice of the girl himself, Mr. Jarvis left the room, upon which his wife flung herself into an easy chair, and putting on a look of the most frigid virtue, she said,—"Come here, child, I want to speak to you."

Marianna approached half timidly, and yet with a look of ingenuous confidence that ought to have ensured esteem.

"I don't know whether you're old enough to understand," said Mrs. Jarvis, "but you have really no business in the world at all; but, as you are to stay here, it is highly necessary you should understand what you're to be, if we condescend to keep you: you're not

to presume ever to come into the room when there's company—
you must be humble and submissive, for, if you're not, you won't
suit us; and if you are asked any questions as to who you are or
what you are, you must say you are a poor orphan kept by the
charity of Mrs. Jarvis—you understand that—one is not going to
feed paupers and have no credit for it."

"She won't say any such thing," said Selina; "you know these
kind of people are always as ungrateful as they can be."

"I shall not say so," said Marianna, "because I am content to
go back from where I came, and where no such reproaches were
cast upon me. I have been taunted by some who were unfeeling,
and who have spoken unkindly of my poor mother, but they were
not all who did so."

"No, indeed, you will not go back. I think it's a very good
thing you have come here, for there's no knowing what notions
might have been put into your head sooner or later—so here you
remain, and your position will be comfortable or uncomfortable
according as you behave yourself—don't stare at me in that manner, child; I don't choose to be looked at in that way—so, understand me, will you now, once for all, speak when you're spoken to,
and not before, and mind what you say to strangers? I really don't
know, Selina, what to do with her as regards where she is to sit."

"We shan't be here long," said Selina, "but while we are,
she'd better have the little back attic, and she can sit there, it's
lively enough, and there she'll be out of the way."

"Well, then, you'd better tell Susan to show her, and there'll be
an end of that job; she can go down to the kitchen to her meals, and
needn't give anybody any trouble."

"Why am I thus treated?" said the girl; "why am I forced to
submit to this degradation? I am not used to it."

"Then you must make yourself used to it," cried Mrs. Jarvis,
as she rang the bell violently; "practice makes perfect, you know:
here, Susan, take this little beggar with you into the kitchen—she
is to stay with us out of charity."

"Lor," says Susan, "what a miracle of goodness you must
be! why, there isn't one in a thousand would do such a thing
or love nor money."

Chapter XI.

MR. BLOOMENBACK ACCOMMODATES
THE FAMILY.

I T was rather tempting for Mr.
Bloomenback to take the larger

share of the cheque which he went to get cashed for himself, but he looked upon the Jarvises as such a good property, that, upon consideration, he scarcely thought there was any occasion to depart from his word, and accordingly he did forward £3,000 out of the cheque to Rhododenderon Jarvis.

But still there was something which now and then kept crossing the mind of the attorney that made him uneasy, and of so undefined a character was that something, that if Mr. Bloomenback had been put upon his oath to describe it—not that we consider that gentleman's oath would have made any material difference in any testimony he might have to give upon any particular subject—he would have been at a loss to say what it was he dreaded.

It seemed as if the shadow of some coming evil was resting upon his soul—a shadow that he could not define—a shadow which was becoming, each moment, deeper and deeper still, and more serious in its density, without being a bit more explanatory.

In vain he kept telling himself that all must be right, and that no possible hitch could occur in the business; he still had a disagreeable presentiment that all was wrong, and had there been the least difficulty made on the part of Mr. Gage with respect to the five thousand pounds, that suspicion would have become almost a certainty; but when he saw the money parted with so easily, he began to think it the next thing to impossible that aught could be amiss, and yet he was uneasy.

He repaired to his chambers and shut himself up, with a determination to think as closely and as accurately as he could over the circumstances, but he was not suffered for a long time to be alone, and a knock at his door announced a visitor. So popular a man as Mr. Bloomenback was not likely to be deserted for a very long period of time, and a rap at the door of his chambers soon announced some one in the shape of plaintiff or defendant.

" Confound them," he muttered, "who is that, I wonder, coming to disturb me at a time when I would most gladly be left alone to my own thoughts?"

Before he could reach the door, then, it was clear that, be the visitor whom he might, he was not one of the most patient order of beings, for he knocked again with greater vehemence than before. At length Mr. Bloomenback flung the door wide open, and saw upon the threshold a personage of whom he knew nothing, but whose appearance certainly did not prepossess the attorney in his favour.

There was an affected air of juvenile rakish swagger about the individual that did not suit the views of Bloomenback. The coat collar was turned extravagantly far back; the cuffs were hidden by false wristbands, that threatened to come nearly up to his elbow, and he wore straw-coloured kids, with a hole in the tip of each finger.

His hat was put on a little one-sided, and, indeed, to take him all-in-all, he was just the sort of person the lawyer not only did not wish to see his like again, but never wished to see at all.

"Well, sir!" said Bloomenback, in not the most inviting manner in the world.

"Pretty well, thank you," said the stranger. "Is the genius of evil within—the ensnarer—the eighty-pennyworth of rascality, eh? Is he at home? Is the spider in any corner of his web?"

Mr. Bloomenback started back, as well he might, at this extraordinary address, and began to have serious apprehensions that he had admitted a maniac to the place.

"What do you mean?" he said. "Come, come, be quick!" and then, having heard of such things, Mr. Bloomenback tried to "fix him with his glistening eye."

"Oh! stuff," said the stranger; "don't you pretend to be so jolly green. In the common language of every-day mortals, I want Bloomenback."

"Then, why did you not say so at once, without all this nonsense? My name is Bloomenback; and now, sir, what may you please to want with me, for my time is precious?"

"A private conference, old boy. Your time is only precious in so far as you make money by it. Good! I have come to show you a plan for the accomplishment of that object. You shall be my Orestes, and I your Pylades."

"Indeed!"

"Yes, indeed! Bloomenback; and, if you will lend me your ears for a brief space, I will show you how you may drop into an amazing good thing."

There was something, at all events, sufficiently business-like in this proposition to attract the attention of the attorney, and he said,—"Well, sir, if that is the case, walk in, and I have only to request that you will be as brief as you possibly can."

"Brevity," said the stranger, as he seated himself in Mr. Bloomenback's private room, "brevity, sir, is not always the soul of wit. You see this hat?"

(The lawyer's attention had been rather attracted by the hat, which had evidently seen the nap of better days, but was now most sadly in the sere and yellow leaf.)

"You see this hat, sir; and probably you are a little surprised at a man of my general appearance wearing such a castor; but, knowing you will not let it go any further, I don't mind telling you it is a bet—a wager, sir, between me and my friend Lord Huntforpower who should wear the oldest hat. A cool thousand depends upon it. You see now the reason, and are not at all surprised!"

"Not in the least; I thought it was a matter of taste."

"Ha! ha! Yes, in a manner of speaking, one may say it is."

"May I trouble you to come to the point, sir, and to tell me, in the first instance, who you are?"

"Oh! certainly—yes, yes, of course; how very remiss of me, to be sure! but so many people know me that I thought you might. I am—but my card will illuminate."

The stranger produced a not very clean card, which duly informed Mr. Bloomenback that his visitor was the Honourable Colonel Markham De Mildmay; to which piece of information the attorney's only reply was, "Oh!"

The honourable gentleman seemed rather disappointed that his card had produced no greater a sensation, but he hastily now proceeded to state the object of his visit.

"I intend, Mr. What's-your-name, to put a thousand pounds in your way. There was a gipsy, who predicted that I was to make my fortune by marriage. Well, I have no objection. My—what shall I call him—my humble friend Brown, a hatter, called upon me in the Albany a short time ago, and told me that a Selina Jarvis, in some strange place in the City, would have plenty of tin. Well, he went on to state that you was the confidential lawyer of the family, and, without saying anything to him about it, a happy idea struck me, that I would give you a thousand pounds for an introduction to the rich fair one."

"Oh! indeed; and did it not strike you that I might, by some remote possibility, refuse?"

"Not at all! You are a lawyer, and you know the value of money. I offer a thousand pounds down for the introduction. In two months I am the husband of the female Jarvis, as safe as bricks."

"You are confident, sir."

"Always was."

"So I should say, by your manner and bearing; but, as you offer a thousand pounds down, I confess the matter is worth the looking to. It can't be of any real consequence to me who marries Selina Jarvis, and, if anything is to be made by the transaction, I don't see why I should not make it."

"Most sensibly spoken—spoken like an oracle!"

"Well, sir, you shall have the introduction you want. I presume I may take it for granted, you are what you represent yourself to be? I need make no inquiries, I presume; but if the Jarvises should, I suppose the answers will be satisfactory. I merely spoke, however. Although you have not mentioned it, I am inclined to think you have some other wagers connected with the whole of your costume similar to the one about your hat."

"Ha! ha! Very good, very good! You are quite facetious. The fact is, that, owing to a difference in religious sentiments with the noble family whose name I bear, they have tried to make out, from time to time, that I don't bear it at all. Very wrong of them; but I say always, let me have liberty of conscience above anything. Upon the whole, however, I should say that inquiries would be injudicious, for you can have no conception, Mr. Eighty-pence, what religious rancour will induce people to do."

"Oh yes, I have."

"Well, then, you can understand my position?"

"Perfectly. Are you going to give me a cheque for the thousand?"

"Yes, or the same thing—something of the same value—my bill. My bill, you know, is the same as my cheque."

"Exactly the same; and your cheque is equally valuable as your bill. Now, Mr. Mildmay, or whatever else is really your name, you are a penniless, audacious adventurer, and you want to better your fortunes by marriage. How you could for one moment fancy I could be so green as to be taken in by your pictures, is to me amazing. Don't interrupt me. I hate Selina Jarvis. If you can marry her, do so. You have my best wishes. Deceive her, if you can, and I shall be quite well repaid for any little trouble the matter costs me by a contemplation of her bitter disappointment."

"You are one of the most facetious fellows I ever met with."

"Never mind about that; I am what I am. We understand each other. I will take your bill for a thousand pounds, payable two months hence. If you do succeed, you can pay me; if you do not, you need not trouble yourself about it. I don't throw away a half-sheet of draft paper upon such as you."

"Oh!"

"Leave the matter of the introduction to me; I will manage it naturally, and you shall have a clear stage. Marry her, if you can."

"You may depend upon that. Let me see, I am going now to call upon my friend the Honourable Augustus Fitzdarcy. I—I—dear me, how odd! I have left my purse at home."

"Stop," said Bloomenback, "I would not give you a sixpence to save you from being hung. I merely made that statement because I knew you were about to wind up what you were saying by a request for a loan. You may, therefore, spare yourself all that trouble."

"Oh! God bless me! you don't call half a sovereign a loan, do you?"

" Yes."

" Then you rather won't?"

" I positively won't."

" Then I can tell you that you are very ridiculous, Mr. Eighty-pence. Who is a gentleman to get money of, if not of his solicitor —his man of business? I can offer you a mortgage, sir, as a matter of course—a mortgage which must be redeemed—the mortgage of my word of honour. There's security; but if you have made up your mind to do the unamiable, why, I can't help it."

" Not in the least. Good morning! I will write to you when I want you. What is your number in the Albany?"

" Oh! my number! why, I—I have no particular number just at present; but I am always in the passage between two and half-past, you see. If you want to drop me a note, send it to the post-office in Fetter-lane, to be left till called for."

" Very well. Now, once more, sir, good morning."

" Stop; let me see, you will want a stamp for my thousand pounds bill; that I must pay. Just till I see you again, oblige me with five shillings?"

" No, no, no! I contract for my stamps, and pay once a quarter; besides, as I am to receive the money, I insist upon paying for the stamp myself."

" The devil!" muttered the honourable gentleman. " It's no go—not the shadow of a go. Sir, I have the happiness to wish you a remarkably good morning. Hilloa! can't you see where you are going, sir? Upon my honour, I—I——"

These words were addressed to no less a personage than Hannibal Jarvis, who was coming up the narrow, dark staircase, leading to Mr. Bloomenback's chambers, just as the illustrious visitor was going down, and the two gentlemen came rather closely in contact with each other.

" Oh! I beg your pardon," said Hannibal, " I didn't see anybody. I—I aint very well, sir."

" Oh! never mind," cried Bloomenback; " allow me to introduce you, gentlemen:—Mr. Jarvis, this is the Honourable Colonel Markham De Mildmay."

Hannibal made a bungling bow, and the honourable gentleman, seizing his hands, swore a great many oaths, to the effect of how he had heard of him. "Hannibal Jarvis! I absolutely longed to know him, and meet him at clubs and in saloons."

"Oh, you are very kind, sir," said Hannibal, who was quite dazzled with the sounding names and title of the gentleman, "anywhere you please."

"To-night, then, my dear fellow, at nine o'clock, at—let me see, Fouillade's, by the Opera. Ta, ta! good day, Eighty-pence. My cab, I dare say, is somewhere near."

CHAPTER XI.

A FLAW IN THE DOCUMENT.

"REALLY," said Hannibal Jarvis, as he sat down in the chair which the colonel had so recently vacated, "I hadn't an idea you had such great connexions, Mr. B. That's a tip-top sort of fellow, and no mistake."

"Oh, yes; but what's the matter with you? You seem most terribly out of sorts to-day. Why, you look as if you had been ill a month, and had only just crawled out."

"I have only just crawled out," said Hannibal, with a groan; "you are right enough, so far as that goes, Mr. B. Do you know, I don't think, somehow, that bottled stout mixes up well with sherry?"

"I don't think it does; what are you rolling your head about so for? Is it to try and delude me into a belief that there's anything in it?"

"Oh, don't joke, it's cruel; if you had such a headache as I have, you would go out of your senses. I can hardly see out of my eyes, and that's how I came to run against that nob on your staircase; I hope that I shall be well enough to meet him, that I do."

"Oh, you will be all right. What have you been doing?"

"Sick for the last six hours or so, and coming it fast before that; I—I am ready to drop now."

"But, why don't you try to take something? A little fat bacon, now, anything oily, rich, and unctuous might do."

"Oh no, no; do you want to kill me, B.? You have made me ten times worse with the very thoughts, you have. Oh, my head, what shall I do! Can't you advise me? You must have done the fast thing, surely, some time or another. What are you looking for? don't show me anything fat to eat, whatever you do, B. Have mercy upon me!"

The attorney went to the cupboard, where he kept the suspicious looking bottle, and poured out a brimming glass of brandy, in one of those capacious rummer glasses now so little used. He then procured a light with a lucifer match, and, to the surprise of Hannibal, he set the top of the spirit in a flame, and let it burn for a few moments with a pale blue flame. Then he put it out by placing above it for a moment a piece of slate to exclude the air.

About a fourth part of what he had poured out into the glass was consumed, and then handing what remained to Hannibal, said,—
" Toss that off, and in ten minutes you will feel yourself a new man."

" You don't say so ?" said Hannibal, as he took the glass in his trembling hand, and eagerly drank off the contents.

"Yes, and now to business. You have not come here for nothing."

" No, no. The fact is a man can't be fast without money, you know, that's impossible; and I thought you might put me in the way of getting a little accommodation, just now, as it will be some time, perhaps, before I can get the governor to bleed as he ought to do."

" Well, Hannibal, I may, perhaps, be able to do what you wish: you are twenty-one, I think?"

"Yes, last birth-day."

"Then how much do you want?"

"A couple of hundred. I don't mind what I pay for them; for the real fact is, I cannot do without them, and no mistake;

I lost some money last night at Blind Hookey, and I haven't got a rap in the world."

"Very well; I will, on your acceptance for three hundred pounds at two months, let you have a cheque for two hundred pounds."

"Give us hold of it: upon my word, I don't know whether it's your burnt brandy, or the prospect of the tin; but I do feel wonderfully better, and my head is not throbbing away in that horrible and desperate manner it was."

"It's the burnt brandy; and now you know what to do, if you go a little too fast, another time, Hannibal; just run out and buy a stamp, and I will accommodate you with the cash you want, and you must work it out of the governor, you know."

"Leave me alone for getting it, and I shan't say anything to the governor. It's the old woman I'll get it of, and no mistake. Oh, I'm getting all right again now, I can almost shake my head, and I could not have done so ten minutes ago for a twenty-pound note."

"No doubt; be off with you now, as quick as you can, and get the stamp. I can't be waiting here all day; and I have now some out-of-door business to transact."

Hannibal soon procured the stamp, and, in the course of another five minutes, he had a cheque of Mr. Bloomenback's in his pocket.

"Upon my word," he said, as he drew up his shirt collar, and settled his chin into his cravat, "I'm much obliged to you, for I was regularly stumped, and no mistake. I say, I suppose that nob I met here will keep his appointment."

"Certainly; and I will let you into a secret. He admires Selina."

"Selina—what, my sister! There's no accounting for tastes. Come, you don't mean that, B., do you now?"

"Yes, I do; and if you be of any assistance to him, he will introduce you to all the nobility, and the tip-top, highflying fast fellows upon town, so he tells me. You can therefore use your own discretion in the matter; I leave it and him entirely in your hands."

" Oh, thank you, thank you! I really am much obliged. I'm forced to be off. Good day."

" You need make no apologies; I'm only too glad to get rid of you," said Bloomenback. " There's a knock, too, at my outer door, so, as we have transacted all our business, good day to you, Master Hannibal."

Hannibal left the chamber, and Mr. Bloomenback admitted a brother professional from the inn, who came upon business by no means essential to the progress of our story.

And while these vicious men were scheming and plotting, the one with the other, about their conflicting interests, how cheerless and how wretched did poor Marianna Brotherton feel in the house of the Jarvises! From what has been hinted from time to time, by the different personages connected with our story, the peculiar position of Marianna may be understood.

When old Mr. Bootle was informed by his beloved daughter, Lucinda, that she had, without his consent, married Lieutenant Brotherton, his indignation was greatly roused; but not so greatly as to shut the door upon all possibility of reconciliation. It is true that, in his first flush of anger, he banished his daughter from his house and presence; but both she and her husband considered that, when calmer reflections came, he would accord his forgiveness.

It was not so much the marriage that he was angry at, as the fact of the secrecy with which it had been contracted; but if he had reasoned correctly upon the matter, he would have found that he had himself only to blame for that, inasmuch as he had extorted from one, who might be called a mere child, when she made her promise, an engagement that she would not wed while he lived.

It was the violation of this pledge which made old Bootle so angry, although, from the mere fact of it having been entered into, any man of the world would have augured, sooner or later, a secret marriage on the part of Lucinda.

The old man obstinately rejected all communication with his daughter or her husband, who, it happened, in the midst of all this, was ordered to India with his regiment. The heart of old Bootle was oeginning to soften, when the Jarvises came to him to tell him, that not only had his daughter, contrary to the pledge she had entered into, left him, but she was not even married to the man for whom she had deserted him.

This was just a week before Lieutenant Brotherton started for India; and the most singular part of the whole affair was, that no less than three persons, who were employed by the old man to call upon him, saw him and a lady, whom he said was his wife, and who was not Lucinda.

Then it was found that there was no entry in the parish registry of the church, at which Lucinda had said she was married at, of any such circumstance having taken place; and she alleged that she had lost the certificate, but produced a letter from her husband, asseverating, in the most solemn terms, that she was his wife, and stating that only two persons, namely the clergyman and the parish clerk, were present at the marriage, and that they were both dead, and he could not account for the absence of an entry in the church registry of the marriage.

Confused and confounded by all these conflicting circumstances and apparent evidences, the old man was led to believe by the Jarvises that one of the grossest attempts ever heard of was being made to deceive him, and he solemnly cast his child for ever from his heart. He shut himself up in the Priory, and for some time refused to see anybody but his old gardener, although, at length, he did reconcile himself to the presence of Mrs. Green, his housekeeper. And the most surprising thing of all was, that Mr. Gage was one of the parties who had called upon Lieutenant Brotherton in London, and ascertained that he was residing with a female he called his wife, but who was not Lucinda Bootle. If she were with him at all, she must be his mistress.

And thus the matter rested. The lieutenant went to India, Lucinda disappeared, and for eight years the old man led the life of a misanthrope, determining upon and actually leaving by will all his property to the Jarvises.

was one calm sweet summer's eve that Mr. Gage rode up the long avenue of the Priory to visit his old friend and client, about six months before the events of our story began.

The distant rays of the setting sun shone through the foliage of that noble avenue of trees with a pleasant lustre, but the attorney was certainly too deep in thought to pay much attention to the beauties of the scenery by which he was surrounded. He trotted his horse up to the house, till he was met by the old gardener, who knew him well, and who, in answer to his inquiries about his master, shook his head, saying,—

" Well, I hardly know, Mr. Gage. He wants a deal of propping up, sir. I'm afraid he won't blossom no more. He's like a piece of dead wood, sir. I don't think all the care in the world will do him any good. He's agoing, sir, at the roots—that's my opinion, Mr. Gage, and he won't stand the winter."

" You think not ?"

" Not I, sir. I know what plants is, and human *beans* is something like 'em, sir."

" Well, just tell him I'm here."

" Oh ! you know you can go in, sir. I'll take care o' your horse. You'll find the precious old evergreen in the little room where he always sits."

Mr. Gage knew that room well; and there, sure enough, he found the old man, who gave him a calm and kindly welcome, although it was evident, from his manner, that sorrow and he had been long familiar.

After a time the old man seemed to be aware that the attorney had something upon his mind, and he looked earnestly at him, as though he would have said, " Speak, I am here to listen."

" Mr. Bootle," said Gage, " I am about to speak to you upon an interdicted subject, but it is absolutely necessary that you should know that which I have to say concerning it."

" Go on, go on."

" Your daughter's husband is no more."

" Well?"

" She likewise has been taken to the tomb."

The old man's lips moved, but he uttered no sound. He shook like an aspen leaf.

E

"You are not childless," added the attorney. "Lucinda has left a child. Will you take it to your heart? It, at least, is innocent."

"Base-born!" gasped the old man—"base-born! I—I—will not see it—I cannot. Let—let it have enough, but never cross my path. Lucinda! Lucinda!"

A gush of tears came to his relief, and when that burst of feeling had subsided, Mr. Gage spoke to him again, saying,—

"Mr. Bootle, since you have made your will, and left every thing to the Jarvises, I have caused the most careful inquiries to be made concerning them. The result of those inquiries is not favourable. They are ascertained to be selfish and bad people, and without the smallest vestige of that affectionate feeling for which you have given them credit. The man Bloomenback, too, is one of those who bring discredit upon what ought to be an honourable profession."

"Does all that alter one fact?"

"It ought to alter one fact; and that is, the fact of your leaving all your property to them."

"Do you want it?"

"No; I am an independent man, as you know, and don't want it. But I should like to see you make a better use of it. If you were dead to-morrow, those Jarvises would soon show you what they really are. They would then unmask, and you would know them. Now, Mr. Bootle, you have had reason to trust me often, and you have never had that trust betrayed. You have often said you would be glad to do me some favour. Will you allow me to persuade the Jarvises that you are dead, and see what they will do? Leave the orphan child to their care, and let that be the test."

"Be it so; and, mind you, every farthing of my supposed bequest that they make a good and kindly use of, they shall receive from me in cash at once when the cheat is discovered. If they are what you say, I shall make a new will. Manage it all as you please."

It was thus that Mr. Gage got a *carte blanche* from old Mr. Bootle to test the sincerity of the Jarvises, and he had other views besides, for he began to believe that Lucinda had been married.

CHAPTER XII.

MR. SMITH'S COMMUNICATION.

WITH the assistance of the short explanation which we have now made, the reader will be well enabled to understand all the difficulties that stood in the way of Mr. Gage in confounding the knavish tricks of the Jarvises.

We have said that he began to believe, almost despite the evidence of his own senses to the contrary, that Lucinda Bootle had been really and duly made the wife of Lieutenant Brotherton, and he thought that there was some mystery connected with the affair, which, if anybody knew all about, that body was Mr. Jarvis, and perchance, likewise, his great friend and adviser, Mr. Bloomenback.

E 2

After he had received such unlimited powers of action from Mr.
Bootle, Mr. Gage returned to town, and then commenced the series
of circumstances which we have partially detailed, and which had
so completely imposed upon the Jarvises, and even hoodwinked
the sagacity of no less a cunning personage than Mr. Bloomenback
himself.

But the main plot had not yet commenced, and such an experiment was to be made upon the cupidity of the Jarvises as Mr.
Gage fully expected would exhibit them in such a light as could
not fail to open the eyes of old Mr. Bootle at once to their
character, if it did not establish another object more important
still—namely, the complete justification of Lucinda.

Three days have elapsed. The drysaltery business has been
neglected; an immense house at the west end of the town is
taken, ready furnished, by the Jarvises; Mrs. Jarvis has her own
chariot nearly ready, and Mr. Hannibal has already been twice
thrown sprawling out of his cab; Miss Selina is smitten with the
Honourable Colonel Mildmay, who has won enough money of young
Jarvis to appear in the tip-top style of fashion at the new house of
the family.

Everything, as the novelists say, looks *couleur de rose*, and it
seems quite impossible that anything now can mar the greatness
of the Jarvises. Mrs. J. has issued cards for an evening party,
the first and last to which she intends to invite all her City friends.
She wants to dazzle them all for once, to arouse every spark of
envy in their dispositions, and then to have done with them for
ever. She don't mind their finding out afterwards what they were
that once invited for. Amiable creature!

This entertainment is to be on a scale of great magnificence:
it is to cost five hundred pounds, and nothing is to be spared that
can dazzle and excite the most envious feelings of all who come to
it. There is to be Mrs. Smallbones, of course, the draper's wife
—indeed, every Mrs., who from time to time in the city of
London had attempted to wage a war in the shape of dress,
appearance, and evening parties with the Jarvises, was to be
nvited on that one absolutely crushing occasion. She knew—did

Mrs Jarvis—that they would go home positively ill, but that was just what she wanted.

It was quite clear that Mrs. Jarvis understood the philosophy of wealth, and it was equally clear that Miss Selina shared that knowledge with her ; and the principle that they both so urgently insisted upon, to the effect of " What's the use of being well off unless it aggravates other people !" was, perhaps, the most cordial point of agreement that had ever shown itself in their characters; on many another point they were strictly at variance.

And Mr. Jarvis shared a little in this feeling : if he had not, it is not to be supposed that he would so readily have given his consent to the proposition of astonishing his City friends, at so serious a cost to himself. He felt that it would be a gratification, and an intense one too, to see the stare of his City friends at all the grandeur with which he could surround himself; how gratifying it would be to show Alderman Something, who had not thought him, Mr. Jarvis, good enough—*i.e.* rich enough—to be his associate, that he could outdazzle a Lord Mayor, if he chose ; and that he could make his *fetes* and entertainments such, that if people came not to him from affection, they most unquestionably would from wonder, and because it would be sure to be the fashion to go to a man's house, who did not care if he spent £500 in an evening in the entertainment of a few friends.

And then Selina did not stop to question whether the passion of the Honourable Colonel Mildmay was a new or an old feeling, it was quite sufficient for her that it was, or seemed to be, serious.

The vanity of the brother had induced him to puff off his new acquaintance to the very echo, so that Mr. Bloomenback had no trouble whatever in introducing to the Jarvises the adventurer, whom he hoped to see so thoroughly deceive them; and the idea of becoming Lady Selina Mildmay was quite sufficiently dazzling, both to Mrs. Jarvis and her daughter, to induce them to overlook any minor imperfections in the gallant colonel.

It was true that he had a slight propensity to what he called walking into old Jarvis's wine, so that certainly the honourable gentleman, during the few days he had been an acquaintance of the Jarvises, had certainly upon several occasions taken the extra glass. Then, again, he had a slight propensity to borrow sovereigns; but these were imperfections which, like the spots in the sun, Selina would not suffer herself to think upon as detracting by any means largely from the merits of one who seemed disposed to place her in such juxtaposition with the Peerage.

Of course, all these matters made a tolerable hole in Mr. Gage's cheque, and the Jarvis' family began to find out how very easy it was to spend £15,000 a year, seeing that, in about one week, they were more than half through a third of that amount.

But then, as Mrs. Jarvis remarked, " those were expenses not likely to occur again, and not at all in the regular order of things." Of course, she wanted jewels, and so did Selina ; then their dress-maker's bill was by no means a jocular affair ; and then there was the money paid down to go into the furnished house in Park-lane ; there was the coach-maker's account, too ; so that, with one thing and another, the thousands soon dwindled to hundreds.

Mr. Jarvis winced a little at these proceedings; he seemed to think that, like Hannibal, they were all going a little too fast, but he was cajoled out of any opposition by his wife and daughter.

Certainly, on the eve of the grand entertainment, as he glanced around him in the splendid apartments, and saw them so brilliantly lit with such a profusion of wax candles, and felt really how splendid that place looked which called him master, he did not grudge the sum which had been expended in making it what it was.

"Certainly," he said, "the money has flown, but there is something to show for it, there can be no doubt of that; and if this entertainment does cost £500, I shall have a thousand pounds worth of gratification in seeing the ill-suppressed envy of my City friends."

" Undoubtedly you will," said Mrs. Jarvis. " Don't you feel already a different man to what you did ? Come here, and just look at this inner room—there ! it cost fifty pounds in Common-garden for those exotics."

" Exotics ! exotics ! for God's sake don't make such a blunder as that—the effect, certainly, is fine."

"Then come this way," said Mrs. Jarvis, laying hold of him again by the cuff of his coat, "and I'll show you the eatables and drinkables room."

"The refreshment-room—cannot you call it the refreshment-room? You will spoil everything if you're not choice in your forms and modes of expressions."

"Well, well, I'll be careful; but, as I'm alive, look there—did you ever?"

"Did I ever what? What do you mean?"

"Why, as I'm a sinner, there's Job Brick and the little bastard sitting in the corner all among the plants and the flowers, and talking together as if they'd known each other for a hundred years. I'll soon put a stop to that."

"Hush!—no, no, no—let them be—not yet—we must do nothing yet. The time will come when all that can be arranged properly; but not now, not now; that child, for some reason or another, has struck up a friendship with the boy."

"I'll just say a word to her for all that," exclaimed Mrs. Jarvis; and she would have rushed forward, but her husband's arm detained her, and at the same moment a thundering peel at the street-door announced the first arrival of the visitors, whom it was the especial object of the Jarvises to astonish.

In another moment Mrs. Jarvis had forgotten the very existence of Marianna Brotherton, for Mrs. Deputy Peacock had just arrived, and had actually met Mrs. Smallbones, the draper's wife, on the steps of the door.

But these ladies seemed to be fully alive to the kindly intentions of their hostess, for they wouldn't of their own accord look at anything, and whatever was forced upon their attention, they would not be astonished at on any account whatever.

"In a little time," said Mrs. Jarvis, with a toss of her head, "we shall get things more to rights; but tradespeople are so dilatory, so you must excuse what's wanting, and just put up with this humble sort of place at present."

Now, there could be no doubt that a thousand pounds would not have purchased the moveable articles in the humble apartment where these words were spoken, and the ladies knew that perfectly well, for they were pretty good judges of all that sort f thing; but truly there are none so blind as those who will not see, and that was about the predicament in which the two City dames were.

" Oh!" said Mrs. Smallbones, " don't make any excuse, don't say a word about it; it's not of the least consequence. I really dare say we shall do very well; and, as you remark, you'll get more settled in time."

' Oh, dear, yes!" said Mrs. Deputy Peacock—" certainly. There can be no question about that, and as it is, I think you may make yourself very comfortable; of course, everything can't be done in a minute."

Mrs. Jarvis bit her lips, for she thought and knew the place was perfect. She gave that irritated sort of giggle which people do frequently when they wish to affect mirth under the most unmirthful feelings.

" How very kind of you," she said, " to try and reconcile me to the place! We have not had time to spend yet above two or three thousand pounds upon it; but, of course, that's nothing to us, though it would ruin most people."

" Dear me! so it would; but I suppose you get long credit?" said Mrs. Smallbones.

" No; we prefer paying for what we have, particularly in drapers' goods; they are such wretches and thieves—the present company always excepted, Mrs. Smallbones."

" Oh dear! don't mention it! I always myself thought the drapers nearly as bad as the drysalters."

" But worse than all that—don't you think," said Mrs. Deputy Peacock, " is a beggar on horseback?"

" Oh, dear, yes! most certainly."

" Very good, very good," said Mrs. Jarvis; and at that moment she could have eaten her two dear friends with the smallest possible amount of salt—" very good, indeed. By-the-by, Mrs. Deputy Peacock, they say your husband never will be anything in the City of any consequence, on account of his ignorance, and having some time ago compounded with his creditors."

And in this sort of way did the ladies amuse each other until the arrival of other guests made the conversation more general and discursive. The saloons were soon full of, as far as dress went, good company. The Honourable Colonel Mildmay was there, in all his glory, and at eleven o'clock a space was cleared for quadrilles, while a private band, certainly of excellent musicians, struck up a triumphal strain of music as a commencement to the amusements of the evening.

It was just about then that Mr. Gage, who had been invited, crept up to Mr. Jarvis, and whispered into his ear,—

" I have had a letter from Mr. Smith."

————

CHAPTER XIII.

THE CHANGED PROSPECTS.

Of course Mr. Jarvis expected that Mr. Smith, who, he was told, had Mr. Bootle's will in his possession, would write immediately in answer to Mr. Gage, and then that gentleman would likewise, of course, lose no time in communicating with him, Mr. Jarvis.

This was all in the natural order of things, and to be expected; but there was something in the tone and manner of Mr. Gage that terrified Jarvis, and made him think that all was not right.

He shook like an aspen leaf as he retreated into the recess of a window, which was shaded by deep crimson curtains, and asked in a tremulous voice for the communication.

" Of course," said Mr. Gage, " you fully expected such communication from me; I have only about two hours' since received his note, for it came through a private channel. He is at Milan; but I will read it to you, and you will be able to judge for yourself how you like it. I should say it was the most satisfactory thing you could meet with."

Mr. Jarvis breathed more freely as he repeated the words "satisfactory thing," and added,—

"Oh, then of course it's all right; he has the will."

"Certainly, most certainly, and acknowledges to the possession. There is his letter, read it for yourself."

"What a fool I was to be frightened!" thought Jarvis, as he drew himself up and protruded his chest; "I need not have been alarmed. Mr. Gage, I thank you for your very polite attention, sir, and the—the promptness with which you have brought me this epistle. Of course, from what you had said to me, I was sure that all was right, only I wished the thing done in a business way."

"Oh, certainly, certainly; read the letter, sir."

Mr. Jarvis opened the letter, and while the crash of music sounded in his ears, blended with the hum of voices and the busy feet of the dancers, he read as follows :—

"'MY DEAR MR. GAGE,—

"'I certainly have Mr. Bootle's will in my possession, and I very much regret to hear of his sudden decease. I fear it may be three weeks yet before I reach England, for you know I have a commission to examine witnesses in a case; but if a copy of the will be of any use to you, pray let me know, and I will send one by return; but I don't like to risk the original document, which is so important to Mr. Jarvis and his family, by post.'"

"Really," said Jarvis, "this is considerate of Mr. Smith, and I can only say that I should be too happy to make that gentleman's acquaintance; it's very considerate of him indeed, Mr. Gage."

"Oh, you will find him a gentleman in every sense of the term; but pray read on, and I'm sure you will come to something that will gratify you, inasmuch as it will take a great weight off your shoulders."

"Thank you, thank you," said Jarvis, and he again composed himself to the perusal of the letter.

"'I don't know, my dear Gage, if you are aware that just before I left England old Mr. Bootle added a codicil to his will.''

How Jarvis shook! A sort of strange rush of blood came to his eyes and ears, and the music sounded dimly, as if at a far distance; he never had felt so faint in all his life.

"Pray, Mr. Jarvis, read on," said Gage, "there's nothing to be alarmed at."

After a minute or two the drysalter sufficiently recovered to continue the perusal of the document.

"'This codicil runs as follows—I give it you literally:—"And whereas, my daughter Lucinda, deceived by a man of the name of Brotherton, gave birth to a child, who I am told is named Marianna (its legal appellation, then, is Marianna Bootle) and to this child I bequeath the sum of twenty-five thousand pounds, to be taken from my real estate.'"

"Damnation!" said Jarvis.

"Sir."

"I—I don't know what to say. Twenty-five thousand pounds to a bastard child! Twenty-five thousand—a fortune!"

"While you have Heaven knows how many times that amount, can you grudge it, Mr. Jarvis?"

"Grudge it, sir! grudge it, sir! I'll dispute it—I'll dispute every shilling of it. I'll be skinned before she shall have it."

"Consider, sir, consider: the income you would derive from the whole of the property of Mr. Bootle would be, in round numbers, fifteen thousand pounds per annum. Suppose, now, this bequest of his to his daughter's child reduces that income to twelve thousand pounds, ought you, sir—I ask you as a man—to complain? As the father of children yourself, I appeal to you."

"She shall have twenty-five thousand drops of my blood first."

"Well, sir, you are made trustee of the whole of the property, and this is the sole legacy; you have the whole of the residue. Now, I tell you plainly, that the next friend of that child shall be found out, a bill shall be filed in chancery, and you know very well you'll never then see a single sixpence of the property, if you were to live till the age of Methuselah."

"Who speaks of chancery?" said Mr. Bloomenback, gliding into the window recess. "Really, gentlemen, gentlemen, I'm sorry to see symptoms of disagreement between you. What can have happened?"

"Oh," said Jarvis, "you've happily arrived, Mr. Bloomenback. Just read this, sir: you know very well that I was told the whole of Mr. Bootle's property was left to me; and now suddenly comes a drawback of twenty-five thousand pounds, quite unknown to Mr. Gage, of course quite unknown, until he had communicated with his dear friend Smith; and yet it's so very funny that this twenty-five thousand pounds should be the precise sum he recommended me to give to this base-born brat: that's funny, very funny, aint it?—damned funny!"

"Hush, hush!" said Mr. Bloomenback, " you astonish me; but you know, my dear Mr. Jarvis, if there be this legacy you must pay it, if it were ever so funny; and, as your legal adviser, I strongly reprobate your making any disturbance about it."

"Ah," said Mr. Gage, "you're a sensible man, Mr. Bloomenback; there's Mr. Smith's letter—you can read it, and see for yourself; and, as I am no dancer, and don't want anything to eat or to drink, I shall bid you good night, gentlemen."

"Bloomenback," said Jarvis, when they were alone, " this is a trick, it's nothing but a trick to get £25,000 out of me to portion off that girl with, but I won't do it—confound the music, I wish they'd stop it, how it jars upon my nerves—and there's Selina, too, dancing with that lump of deformity, Colonel Mildmay, the fellow's an ape, I hate him."

"Why, my dear friend Jarvis, you seem most uncommonly unhappy; come, I have read this codicil, which is here given verbatim in the letter, you shall admit the codicil without question, but you shall not pay one farthing of it."

"How, how?"

"It is left expressly to Marianna Bootle, the illegitimate child of Lucinda Bootle—now there's no such person, for we can prove the legitimacy of that child—we know that she was married to Lieutenant Brotherton—we know where the marriage certificate is—we know where the torn-out leaf from the register is that proves the marriage—we know——"

"Hush! hush! for God's sake don't run on in that way—of course we know enough to transport us both."

"Psha! it can be managed without that—say no more to Gage about it; admit the will, and then advertise for proof of Brotherton's marriage with Lucinda Bootle. I'll take care that somebody answers the advertisement and brings forward the proof, and for that service I require——"

"What?"

"£12,500—halves you know—halves—you get the same—can anything be fairer?"

"Curses on ye all, I'm robbed at every turn. I tell you, Bloomenback, since I've had this money, or been aware that I was to have it, I have not known a moment's peace."

"Oh, that will all pass away—come, come, you must mingle with your guests; how bad it looks for you and I to be whispering in the recess of a window, while everybody else is dancing and doing the amiable."

"That infernal codicil has driven me wild."

"Nonsense, nonsense! we shall beat them yet; leave all that to me—don't I tell you how it can be managed?—come and dance with somebody or another—there, look at Hannibal, did you ever see such extraordinary capers?"

"And all the room laughing at him: there he goes—he falls down and has laid hold of the skirts of his partner's dress."

"Never mind," said Bloomenback, "he's the heir-apparent to £15,000 a year; there's a lively measure—now, isn't that glorious music, did you ever hear the like?—come, Jarvis, all's right."

Bloomenback dragged his reluctant friend into the glare of light of the principal saloon, where, with a forced and sickly smile upon his face, the drysalter tried to make himself agreeable to the people he hated, while his heart was wrung with anxieties, and he knew that there was not one who would not have gloried in the disappointment of his dearest hopes.

CHAPTER XIV.

THE DOUBLE MARRIAGE.

WHILE Mr. Jarvis was thus reaping the fruits of fortune, and heaping up his troubles as he heaped up his riches, his children were certainly enjoying, as far as in them lay, all the advantages derivable from the wealth to which they considered themselves heirs in expectancy.

To the astonishment and delight of Hannibal Jarvis, the Honourable Colonel Mildmay had brought with him a lady, a relation of his own, and therefore quite unimpeachable as regarded manners and virtue—a fair creature, who, as Selina remarked to her brother, evidently had moved in the very best society, for she was abashed at nothing.

She was introduced as the Honourable Miss Georgiana Damer, a cousin of Colonel Mildmay, and such was the fascinating grace of her manners, that she completely won the heart of Hannibal; and when he heard her in a whisper tell her cousin, the colonel, that he, Hannibal, so strongly reminded her of a certain Count Sckrozinski, that, under any other circumstances, she should at once have spoken to him, under the belief that he was that distinguished nobleman, the fascination was complete.

He felt, too, so much at his case in this lady's company, for, if he said the stupidest thing imaginable, she was ready to applaud it as the profoundest piece of wit.

Then, although he floundered through a quadrille in the most awkward manner possible, she praised his dancing, and she hung so fondly on his arm in their route to the supper-room, that he felt, as positive as any human being could feel, that he had most unquestionably smitten that fair and free scion of nobility.

"Ah," she said to him, with a languishing air, that ought to have reminded him of a minor theatre,—"ah, how strange it is, that in my dreams I have often pictured to myself one like you, with whom I could have glided down the stream of time, in the beautiful shallop of felicity!"

"Have you, really!" said Hannibal; "you don't mean it?"

"What a poetical idea," said the lady,—"how sweetly you express yourself!"

"No, no, it's you—it isn't me!"

"Ah, deceiver! how many hearts you have broken!"

Hannibal began to think that perhaps he had, without knowing it.

"I do not know," said the lady, with a sigh, as she fixed her eyes upon the chandelier, and seemed absorbed in thought, "I do not know whether such bright beings do most good or evil in this world; but all that's beautiful must fade away like the blossoms of an hour."

"What a mind she has!" thought Hannibal. "Oh, Honourable Georgiana, can you love?"

"Hush—no more—do not awaken my heart to blissful throbbings—let us speak of your sister, whom Colonel Mildmay adores; she is the polar star of his existence; the bright refulgent beams of which wrap him up like his martial cloak. It was but the other day that the prince spoke to him. 'Mildmay,' he said, 'why don't you settle? Is there nothing fair enough in the court to claim your regard?' "

" 'No, your highness,' was the reply, 'I have made up my mind not to marry until my cousin, Georgiana Damer, can introduce her husband at the Palace.' "

"You don't say so," said Hannibal. "Oh Georgiana, if I might dare to hope!"

"Hope what?"

"That you would be mine!"

"Gracious Heaven! can this be destiny? Is it fate? Are we the victims of a blind chance, to fade away like the cloud-capp'd towers and gorgeous palaces?"

"Oh, Miss Georgiana — excuse me, I mean Honourable Georgiana—if you would but unite your noble fate with mine, then indeed I should say with the poet—I should say with the poet—you can fancy what the poet would say."

"Ah, yes, how eloquent is that broken quotation! Does it not remind one of the fair Ophelia and the willow that grows aslant the brook ? How my heart flutters in its prison-house !"

"She's an angel," thought Hannibal. "The little queen will congratulate me when I'm presented to her at the next drawing-room. Who knows, gracious Heaven ! but I may be made some sort of stick-in-waiting, or usher of something or somebody !"

"Look—look," said the lady ; "do you see how your charming sister hangs upon the arm of the colonel? I will let you into a secret. They have made an appointment to meet to-morrow evening in the gardens of Kensington."

· "Indeed !"

"Yes, they'll sit beneath the shadowy trees, and wonder how the world can be unhappy, while Heaven has left them youth and love."

"But, dear, Honourable Georgiana——"

"Hush! we may be overheard. There's a boy with a sky-blue jacket attending on the guests. I saw him watching us."

"It's that rascal Job Brick; I'll smash him. Heed him not, fair one; but may I hope—oh! tell me that I may hope—you will meet me in Kensington Gardens likewise?"

"I tremble to reply to you; you should not press me; you know that woman's heart is weak."

"No, no, it ain't; meet me to-morrow, or I'll jump into the river."

"Do I hear such dreadful words? It is my fate—at seven o'clock—the Bayswater-gate."

"Oh, delightful!" said Hannibal.

"Hush! no more; they're taking their places for the Lancers: let's dance away the delirium of young joy."

"I have done it," thought Hannibal; "I've won her—evidently the bosom friend of the queen and the admired of all the court—she's mine. I should wonder if the prince don't like it—there's no saying. I won't say anything to the governor about it, I'll be shot if I do!"

While this tender interview was taking place between Hannibal and the Honourable Georgiana Damer, it must not be supposed that the colonel and Selina were quite idle; on the contrary, the gallant officer was making prodigious way.

He had just slightly awakened the jealousy of the lady by bringing his cousin with him; for cousinship is by no means so close a relationship but it may change to something closer still—she was evidently a little piqued, but the assiduous attentions of the colonel soon dissipated the temporary jealousy.

"The fact is, Miss Jarvis," he said, "the dowager countess is too old to go about herself with the Lady Georgiana, and she will not allow her to go anywhere without me; so you see I am forced to play the part of male chaperon to her, and cannot help it; but now let me implore you not to forget your kind appointment for Kensington Gardens."

"No, no; I will not forget."

"Let me hope that I may in time be so blessed as to call you mine. Oh, Selina, I have mingled with the gay throng of many a court; and although," he added to himself, "many a coroneted

brow has flushed at my coming, and I might have chosen a help-
mate among the fair, the proud, the beautiful, yet I looked into my
heart, and I said, ' No, I do not love yet.' "

" Go on, go on."

" But how changed now is everything!   Am I not at once,
paradoxical as it may appear, the happiest and the most miserable
of men?—happy in your society, yet miserable at the idea that
you may not love me as I may wish you to love me."

" Our acquaintance is so very short," said Selina, "and I've not
said anything to my papa."

" Your papa! don't dream of speaking to him.   If I were to
say one word to the earl of a tender attachment, he, looking upon
me as quite booked for one of his nieces, would send me as am-
bassador or plenipotentiary extraordinary to Timbuctoo, and I should
waste away upon Afric's desert shores. Oh, say you will be mine ?'

" I cannot yet—not yet—we will meet to-morrow."

" I say, charming Selina, who is that boy with the sky-blue
jacket, that keeps grinning in my face every minute ?"

" It's Job Brick," said Selina.   " My pa don't like to discharge
him, as he has been with us some time.   But never mind him,
they're making up for the Lancers ; shall we go, colonel ?"

" As you please, heavenly maid."

Mr. Hannibal, too, might be said to be getting on rather fast
now.   How delightful a change had come over the spirit of his
existence !   How very different indeed was his present mode of
life to what it had been, and how completely he felt that all his
genius must have been buried in Bishopsgate-within.

Time was when it was something to have attracted the attention of Deputy Peacock's daughter ; but what a change now had
taken place !   He was actually flirting with an Honourable Lady
Georgiana—with one allied, no doubt, to the highest of the nobility,
—and she had found out his merits—yes, she had actually discovered what a delight it would be to know that she was his.
Oh, happy, happy Hannibal !

A kind of mental intoxication took possession of him, and it
was wonderful to see how he danced, and what extraordinarily new

figures and wonderful steps he insisted upon introducing into every dance. Really Mr. Hannibal got on famously, but not a bit better than his sister, who looked upon herself, to all intents and purposes, as Mrs. Colonel—no, no, the Honourable Lady Mildmay—*that* was it. What a glory it would be to see *that* upon a patent glazed card, and to know that her barouche was continually at the door! No wonder she listened to the honied words of the gallant colonel with abundant pleasure.

And Mrs. Jarvis was not neglected. Somehow or another the kind care of the colonel seemed to spread over the whole of the family, with the exception of the drysalter himself; probably he was considered too dry and intractable to interfere with, but the gallant officer had introduced a certain Sir Thomas Leon, who paid such extraordinary attention to Mrs. Jarvis, that, had she felt fully inclined to exercise the most maternal watchfulness over Selina, she could not have done so.

Sir Thomas led her out to dance—Sir Thomas whispered soft nothings in her ears—he flattered and fooled her to the top of her bent, and never was a whole family so beleaguered as were those Jarvises.

It was quite a treat to see Mrs. Jarvis treading upon everybody's toes, as she went through a quadrille, and it was a greater treat still to see the look of awful contempt with which her City friends regarded her. Probably there was not in the whole of London, on that evening, a party assembled that had about it so many of the elements of discord as that, and yet in which there was so much lip civility.

To hear Mrs. Jarvis and her guests address each other, one would have thought them on upon the most friendly terms that any human beings could possibly be; and yet, a close observer might have detected the hollowness of the smiles, and seen the lurking bitterness beneath every word that was uttered.

As the *Morning Post* said, in giving a description of the entertainment,—" it was not until Aurora showed her golden beams through the windows that the guests separated, leaving those banquet halls deserted, and the charming hostess to the domestic seclusion of her amiable home."

But, before that period came, an explanation had taken place between Selina, the Honourable Georgiana Damer, Hannibal, and the gallant Colonel Mildmay, which ended in the whole four of them agreeing to meet in Kensington Gardens at seven o'clock on the following evening, and it was all but settled that then and there some step was to be agreed upon for securing the permanent happiness of the two couples in the holy bonds of matrimony.

The colonel borrowed £20 of Hannibal, just to show him that he treated him as a friend, and didn't mind letting him know what a close old hunks his uncle, the earl, was, who only allowed him £2,000 per annum, which, of course, did not last him, moving in the circles he did, above three months. How could it?

CHAPTER XV.

THE ARRIVAL AT MR. GAGE'S.

THERE was upon the countenance of Mr. Gage quite a look of calm satisfaction as he left the splendid house of his friends, the Jarvises, after he had delivered the rather uncomfortable epistle of Mr. Smith.

Any one to have seen him, just as he turned away from his short but highly interesting conference with Mr. Jarvis, would have thought him rather in a passion; but, if they had chanced to follow him and observe the quiet smile which lighted up his features when he reached the street, they would certainly have been of a different opinion.

"I think now," he said quietly to himself, "that I have you, Mr Jarvis: your fate and fortune are in your hands, and you are not the sort of man to do yourself any good under the present circumstances, I am convinced, notwithstanding Mr. Bootle's high opinion of you."

He took his way homeward in a well-pleased, contemplative

mood, and, when he reached there, he wrote a long letter to Wilt-shire, detailing all that had occurred, and rather advising than otherwise that he, Mr. Bootle, should come to London and judge for himself as to the prospects the Jarvises had of retaining his good opinion.

After finishing this epistle, Mr. Gage was about to retire to rest, when he was somewhat surprised, considering the lateness the hour, at receiving a card brought in to him by his servant, on which he read, " Mr. Bloomenback, New Inn."

" The gentleman, sir, wishes to see you," said the servant : " I told him you never saw anybody so late, but he said his business was so urgent that he was sure you would not mind."

" Well! show him into my library, and say I shall be with him directly."

In a few moments these two professional personages were to-gether, and a more striking contrast than they were in mind, manners, and disposition surely could not have been found.

Mr. Gage was determined to say as little as possible, and to hear as much as he could, so he merely made a slight bow to his visitor, and requested him to be seated.

" I dare say, sir," said Bloomenback, " you are rather surprised at a visit from me."

" A professional man should be surprised at nothing," said Gage, " and I dare say you have some good and stanch reason, Mr. Bloomenback, for favouring me with this call."

" Why, yes, sir, I trust and believe I have : I have come more as the private friend of all parties, than as the professional adviser of Mr. Jarvis, to say that, as a matter of course, he is, upon con-sideration, very sorry that he suffered himself to say anything intemperate about the codicil to old Mr. Bootle's will, as nothing could really give him more pleasure than in every way fulfilling the intentions of the testator."

" That, of course, is all very proper," said Gage.

" Both I and he, sir, thought it a pity that you should retire to rest to-night under the erroneous impression that Jarvis intended to dispute the codicil—he has no such intention."

"He has been well advised," said Gage.

"Oh yes; but you know when people get angry they always make themselves very ridiculous, sir. For my own part, I very much lament all the unhappy circumstances that have occurred in the family of the Bootles."

"So do I."

"Pray, sir, have you any authentic information of the death of Lucinda Bootle?"

"I heard she was dead, and that consequently the child, as the father had died in India, was an orphan. I recommended it to the care of Mr. Bootle, and I rejoice that he has listened to that recommendation sufficiently to make so handsome a provision for it."

"You are quite right. But, as regards my client, Mr. Jarvis, I can assure you he intended to do something very handsome for the child, indeed."

"Yes, sir; he is a man who says strange things without meaning them,"

"Oh! Is that one of them?"

"What, sir?"

"Why, that he intended to make a handsome provision for the orphan child of Lucinda Bootle."

"Ha! ha!—very good!—very good indeed, upon my word! Oh dear no; but, as you are aware that the mother always declared that she was Lieutenant Brotherton's wife, what a gratifying thing it would be to prove that now!"

"To prove the child legitimate? It would be a gratifying thing to all who know her, and take an interest in her welfare; but I fear there is no chance of such a thing: it is true that Lucinda did always assert that she was married to the lieutenant, but, when it was found that he was actually residing in London with a woman who passed as his wife, and who actually was not Lucinda, old Mr. Bootle became convinced that she had been deceived."

"A-hem!" said Mr. Bloomenback; "you are a professional man, Mr. Gage, and of course want to make as good a thing of the law as you can; now, I have a proposition to make to you."

"I am open to hear it, sir."

"It is just this:—of course my attention, since the death of old Mr. Bootle, has been very much drawn to the circumstances of the case, and Mr. Jarvis has often said to me, 'Bloomenback, I would give any money to prove Marianna legitimate, so that she might take in my family a proper position, without a blemish.'"

"Very kind of him."

"Very kind, as you say.—it was quite a fatherly idea, but then that is accounted for by his having a daughter of his own."

"Exactly."

"Well, then, Mr. Gage, he said he did not mind a couple of thousands spent in the matter. Will you coalesce with me in proving the legitimacy of Marianna, and take one of them?"

"Yes."

"You will? You pass your word?"

"Most certainly I will. Of course I shall be glad to prove the child legitimate, and to make a £1,000 by so doing. How could you doubt it for a moment, Mr. Bloomenback?"

"Well, I—I ought not to have doubted it, of course. I—I— oh no, Mr. Gage—only I asked it as a matter of course, that's all, you know; and now, as all may be considered to have one common object in the matter, I will tell you of a most curious circumstance that came to my own knowledge only lately."

"I will hear you with pleasure."

"I am sure you will. It is this:—A man called upon me some time ago, and said that he would tell me a secret that would sell for something to old Mr. Bootle, of the Priory, Wilts. I looked upon the fellow with suspicion, for he was not exactly that sort of looking individual whom a professional man would like to trust."

"Ah, we are pretty good judges, Mr. Bloomenback."

"Rather; we see something of human nature."

"We do indeed. But what did this stranger say to you, sir? I must own I am a little impatient to hear."

"He said that Lieutenant Brotherton had a brother who was so like him that, unless you saw them together, you could not tell one of them from the other; that there were but twelve months' difference in age between them, but a vast difference in disposition, inasmuch as the brother was a very wild, dissolute sort of man, while the lieutenant was in every respect a gentleman of high honour and integrity."

" Go on, sir, go on."

" I will. This man then went on to state that, just at the period of the elopement—for it amounted to such, unless you may say that Lucinda was turned from her father's house—of Mr. Bootle's daughter, this brother of Lieutenant Brotherton had committed a forgery to a serious amount, and was at hide-and-seek in London, on account of that circumstance, at the very time that the lieutenant and his young wife were at Devizes going by a sham name, and anxiously awaiting the forgiveness of old Mr. Bootle, with whom they corresponded through an acquaintance in London."

" Yes—yes," said Mr. Gage, who, although he would fain have done so, could not conceal the uneasiness he felt, and the deep interest he took in the affair that was being related to him.

" This man," added Bloomenback, " proceeded to tell me that, knowing his remarkable likeness to his brother, Robert Brotherton, which was the name of the forger, took the name of Alexander, which belonged to the lieutenant, and assumed his military title so successfully, that he was actually called upon by the officers of justice several times to inquire if he knew where Robert was, when, as you see, he was Robert himself all the while."

" Yes—yes."

" Well, by that means Robert Brotherton escaped the consequences of his criminality. He was firmly believed to be Lieutenant Brotherton ; and Alexander, this man said, had not the least idea that his brother was personating him in London, but was suddenly surprised at receiving a letter from old Mr. Bootle, up braiding him in the bitterest terms, and declining all further com munication. The fact is, that the old man had, as he thought fully ascertained that the lieutenant was living in London, and a married man before he knew Lucinda ; for Robert Brotherton had his wife with him, and the agents of Bootle had actually called and seen her."

" I understand. Thus by that horrible mistake the old man

thought so unworthily of Lieutenant Brotherton, as to decline any communication with him."

"Exactly—whilst he was all the while living upon the most affectionate terms with his wife Lucinda, in Devizes."

"And why did you not communicate this before?"

"It was only a week before old Bootle's death that I heard it and as I tell you I had my doubts, from the character of the man who came to me, of the accuracy of any statement he might make so I did not feel myself at all authorised to say anything about it until I had made every inquiry; and, before I could do that, I hear that Mr. Bootle is no more. I am, however, now satisfied that the story is correct, and that Robert Brotherton did pass himself off in London as his brother Alexander, to the ruin of all the latter's prospects, as well as the complete destruction of the peace of mind of old Mr. Bootle himself, who now, being unhappily dead, can reap no benefit from the disclosure."

Mr. Gage rose, and paced the room with uneasy strides, as he exclaimed,—

"Good God! and it was I who actually called upon this very Robert Brotherton, on some excuse, and heard him own himself to be Lieutenant Alexander Brotherton, and that a woman of thirty years of age, as different as anything could be from Lucinda, was his wife."

"Oh! was it you?"

"Yes, it was I, who felt it a duty to make every possible inquiry for Mr. Bootle, and who told him finally that I was convinced his daughter had been deceived, although, from many little circumstances since, I have been led to alter my opinion altogether upon that subject."

"Well, sir, I presume now that you are still further inclined to assist me in discovering the legitimacy of Marianna. I will do myself the pleasure of calling upon you to-morrow, when you will have had time to think over the matter, and to advise what had better be done to insure the rescue of the memory of Lucinda from the reproach that now attaches to it."

"Be it so, Mr. Bloomenback, and if you can produce your

informant in this business, and all your proofs, something may be done."

"How odd," thought Bloomenback, as he left Mr. Gage's house, "how odd, that he don't seem at all to see the proof of Marianna's legitimacy deprives her of her £25,000."

CHAPTER XVI.

THE TROUBLESOME AUNT SHUTER.

"Success !" cried Mr. Gage, when he was alone; "success! it is working well. The Jarvises, with the assistance of their counsellor, the attorney of New Inn, will move heaven and earth to prove the legitimacy of Marianna. The legacy has done the business. Oh, the villains ! It was they who gave the address of the sham Alexander, in London, and who, no doubt, knew perfectly well from the first who and what he was. I could almost, now that I know all the affair, take my oath that Bloomenback was Robert Brotherton's attorney, and advised it all."

This was indeed a highly probable supposition.

"And so," thought Mr. Gage, "they think they are deceiving me, and that, in lending them all the aid I can to find out the legitimacy of Marianna, I am depriving her of a fortune. Indeed, cunning Mr. Bloomenback, you must have a great idea of your own penetration, and a very small notion of that of other people's ; but you will be foiled, villain that you are, and little suspect you are forging weapons for your own destruction."

Mr. Gage paused, for to his surprise, at that time of night, he heard the sound of carriage wheels at his door, and then a loud knock upon it, and as violent a ring, denoting the arrival of some important visitor.

He ran down stairs himself, but what was his surprise to see a very aged and immensely big woman, with as much clothing on her as would have done for half a dozen people, being assisted out of a coach.

"Oh, this is a mistake," he cried. "Madam, you are at the wrong house."

"No, no," said a strange, cracked voice; "aint this Lawyer Gage's?"

"Yes, but——"

H.CARTER.

"Get out of the way, you rascal, will you? Oh! my lumbago! —oh—oh—I can walk a little better now—oh! Is Lawyer Gage at home? Ah!"

The old lady walked in, and proceeded to ascend the staircase with all the deliberation in the world, despite the remonstrances of Mr. Gage, who followed her, demanding her name and business with him, till they reached the drawing-room, when the old lady suddenly sunk into a seat, and a voice he knew well said to him, in accents of dejection,—

"Don't you know me, Gage? Is my disguise so perfect, that even *you* fail to discover me?"

"Good God, Mr. Bootle!" exclaimed Mr. Gage, "can I believe my senses? Is this indeed you?"

"Hush! It is! Keep your door close; I could not bear the anxiety of living at a distance while you were about your present operations. I have had a dream—a strange day-dream: I thought I was sitting in my old accustomed seat in the little parlour at the Priory, and my—my child, Lucinda, knelt by me and kissed my hand. I—I heard her say 'God bless him,' as plainly as if I had been awake!"

"You surprise me."

"Yes! yes! It was at the close of yesterday, just as the sun was sinking, and the dim light of eve was creeping on—she—she prayed God to bless me—the pure spirit of my perhaps injured child, 'God bless me!'"

"Mr. Bootle, do not despair. You do not guess what happiness may yet be in store for you, Mr. Bootle; but how came you in this strange disguise?"

"I—I thought it better not to run the least risk of a discovery that my death was a sham, so I found in an old press in the Priory a quantity of clothing belonging to my sister Shuter, and here I am. Oh! it was such a vivid dream: I thought I saw the door open and she glided in, looking paler than I used to know her. She prayed God to bless me, yet I had cast her off from my heart—my child—my poor child!"

"Mr. Bootle," said the lawyer, "this is a great change that has taken place in your feelings, but it is a beautiful change as well—it is one for which you will be all the happier. I am doing my utmost to prove that the Jarvises are unworthy of your regard. Marianna is with them, and she will be able to state all that has passed."

"I must see her as Aunt Shuter: I will call and see her. Is—is she like her mother?"

"The very image; but there is not the serene joyfulness about her that adorned Lucinda: the poor child seems to have inherited grief, but she is very, very beautiful."

" She shall inherit joy."

" You don't know what pleasure you give me, Mr. Bootle, to hear you say that. You must be fatigued by your journey; I will order a bed to be prepared for you."

" No, no, leave me here awhile; my spirits are too much excited to allow me to sleep. If you will sit with me for an hour or so, and tell me all that you have done, I may, perhaps, get some repose, but I am sure I could not just yet."

Mr. Gage himself got some choice wine, which he laid before Mr. Bootle, and then he told the old man all that had transpired and all that he hoped, being, as he proceeded, frequently interrupted by the self-accusatory remarks of Mr. Bootle, and now and then by his tears, as he thought of what his dear child Lucinda had suffered.

The old man gave his warmest approval to the steps that were being taken, and then, as Mr. Gage saw how deeply he was affected, he strove to reassure him, and to turn the conversation to happy channels, by painting to him the future in pleasant colours and telling how happy he might yet be with his grandchild Marianna. Mr. Gage hoped that the old man would retire to rest; but, as he showed no inclination to do so, he resolved to sit up with him as long as he chose, and got another bottle of the choice wine they had been drinking, in order to while away the time; but, observing Mr. Bootle's spirits flagged very much, he said,—

" Come now, sir; I have told you all I can about your affairs, and, as you don't feel sleepy, I will relate to you a little event that occurred to me once."

" Do so, do so," said the old man, " it may distract me from my own thoughts, Gage."

*   *   *   *   *

The lawyer having filled his own and Mr. Bootle's glass, and having executed two or three " hems!" thus commenced his effort to withdraw the old man from too keen a contemplation of his own anxieties.

" By the way," he commenced, " I never told you of my first grand cause—a case in which I was engaged in the earliest part of my professional career. I had very nearly been made the perpetrator of fraud and injustice, and the cause of ruin to others. It was a strange—a very strange affair," he continued, looking thoughtfully at his toes for a minute or more, and then he continued : "I had never before been professionally employed on any matter, save the collection of a few debts by mesne process ; they had been put into my hands by my friends, who were desirous of showing their regard for me, by doing something in the way of setting me agoing in the business of my profession, as I had at that time just entered on my professional career. I was seated one evening before the fire in my private office, gazing on the forms of the flames, as they flickered here and there on the black coals, dodging in and out the bars, as if for their own amusement. Though my eyes were intently fixed upon them, yet I was by no means cognisant of what I saw ; I was paradoxical—I looked, but saw not ; my thoughts were engaged upon a speculation as to how I could enlarge my practice, which had been confined to the cases I have mentioned.

" This was a problem not easily solved.

" The profession of the lawyer and the soldier, I thought to myself, speaking almost aloud, are not unlike in some respects—in one at least—and, yet, unlike that of the divine and the doctor. The former are unlike the latter in this point: they cannot advertise for any share of that business which shall bring them wealth and honour, while the latter can ; but the lawyer must wait for some opportunity when chance or abilities shall give him the position he covets ; in the meanwhile he must wait with calmness, and without complaint, until the desired event shall take place.

" Patience and perseverance are words in everybody's mouth, and uttered upon every occasion, in place or out of place, as if it were a balm that would heal all the wounds inflicted by disappoint-ment ; but still it was peculiarly applicable in my case, for I could exert no other qualities just then. Well, as I was telling you, I sat before my fire, looking without seeing, when a loud double knock came at the door.

" Hilloa ! thought I, what can that mean—an announcement of some friends ? for the idea of its being a business call did not arise in my mind. It was more probably a call of pleasure from some gay companion, who came, doubtlessly, to cheer my hours of idleness and leisure. However, I heard the door open, and my name pronounced by a voice with which I was not familiar. In a minute my clerk entered, to inform me that a gentleman desired to speak to me ; I inquired who he was, and his card, was placed in my hand.

" ' Mr. Robert Smirk,' I read on the card : show him in.

" In half a minute Mr. Smirk entered the office. He was a tall, gentlemanly man, with a keen penetrating glance of the eye, that was peculiarly observable at the first introduction; he bowed slightly, and I (pointing to a seat next my own, on the opposite side of the fire) said,—

" Pray be seated, sir, and inform me in what way I can benefit you; for I had made up my mind that this was a business affair, and began running over in my own imagination the names of my friends, to ascertain, if possible, by that process, which was the most likely among them to have recommended me a client.

" ' I am a stranger to you,' began Mr. Smirk, (I bowed,) and, therefore, my introduction must be as explicit as possible ; and, as it must come from myself, I will be as brief as the nature of my object in coming to you will admit. You have my name—my birth and parentage you will perceive plainly enough, when you obtain the properly authenticated certificate from the proper authorities.'

" ' Pardon me,' said I, ' for one moment; ' interrupting his singular introduction, and wondering in my own mind who could have sent such a man to me,—' pardon me for interrupting you, but who has done me the honour of recommending you to me ? '

" ' The Law List, sir,' he replied ; and seeing, I suppose, my surprise, indicated by my features, he proceeded to say that he was not acquainted with any professional adviser, as he had never before this occasion required the assistance of one. 'Indeed,' he continued, 'I should not now have required one, but from some unaccountable conduct on the part of my brothers and sister, and some friends.'

"I listened to him with some patience and interest, for his manners were calm and gentlemanly, and yet, at times, I detected a keen glance, which I presume was habitual, peering towards me, as if to ascertain by stealth what impression had been made upon me by his words, but this was by no means so palpable as to be intrusive; and he proceeded.

"'You see, sir,' he said, after a few moments' pause, as if he were mentally employed in seeking the best point to begin at, I am the eldest son of a very respectable family, that is, my father, 'when alive, was a man of independent property, and brought up his children as gentlemen, and gave us all a suitable education. Of course we all looked up to him for a decent maintenance, and this was but just, and what was intended by our father. He meant all of us to share his fortune at his death, and while he lived he put us in the best way to appear as gentlemen, and to maintain our position, by giving us the choice of a profession; and, had he lived long enough, would, no doubt, have seen us all flourishing and advancing in our positions with honour and credit.'

"'Certainly,' said I, 'that was the most wise course to pursue, and one calculated to make useful and honourable members in society.'

"'So I think, sir; but he, poor man, is now dead; he has been dead but nine months, and his family are all in disorder—at enmity the one with the other—a scene of heart-burning contention has arisen amongst us, that it would have been impossible to account for on any other ground save that I am the eldest, and that is one reason why my brothers and sisters have all united together against me.'

"'Against you! and why should they do that?' I inquired 'Upon some personal grounds, I suppose; and yet that is difficult' for a stranger to understand.'

"'Yes, it is,' he replied, 'but it is not so when I tell you the matter is easily susceptible of explanation. As I told you, I am the eldest, and when I tell you that my father died intestate, you will no longer wonder at the effect it has produced, that is, in securing enmity against myself.'

" ' Well,' said I, 'that cannot affect you much, except in so far as it must be a very disagreeable thing to be at enmity with one's own kindred: unpleasantness, however, will arise under such circumstances, and all that can be done, is to disarm them of half their strength by meeting them in a conciliatory spirit.'

" ' That is all right enough,' pursued Mr. Smirk, ' but that is not all: I could bear any man's enmity quietly enough, because it could not well eat its way into my soul—I could bear with it as a negative evil, but when it takes the character of and becomes an active and positive mischief, I can no longer tamely endure it.'

" ' Certainly,' I replied, ' all things when they become wrongs ought to be redressed, and in cases where dispute does arise, the law steps in and settles the matter.'

" ' That is the very point, sir,' said Mr. Smirk, ' at which I have arrived myself, and which displays at once in an abstract point of view my position ; but to obtain your aid and advice I must relate the particulars of my case, and then you will perceive I have no common cause of complaint against my brothers and sisters. My father dying intestate has left me of course heir-at-law, and by virtue of that I am entitled to take out letters of administration, and administer to his effects, and enter into possession and enjoyment of all he has left.'

" ' Certainly ; but of course you must allow them their proper share.'

" ' That I am most willing to do, but they are not content with that, but insist on having all among them, and shutting me out from any participation in the benefit to be derived from my father's property—a proceeding you must at once acknowledge not in accordance with either law or equity, and a disposition of affairs that I will not submit to, while I can appeal to a court of justice, and while I am in a position to prove all I have now told you.'

" ' There can be no doubt, if the case is as you have related to me,

I replied, 'you will not have to appeal in vain; but will you permit me to ask you the grounds upon which they attempt to exclude you from a participation in the property left you by the decease of your parent? It is too far beyond my comprehension to make a guess at.'

"'And so it would be for any one else,' he answered. 'They have the impudence and malice to declare that I am not my father's eldest son. They say in fact that I am his son by some one else, and am not entitled to share with them, and that I am an alien in the family, and refuse to have anything to do with me. They have taken possession of everything and defied me. What am I to do? How can I proceed?'

"'By filing a bill in Chancery,' I replied; 'but are you in a position to prove that you are the son of your father—that you were born in wedlock, and that you are the eldest, and in fact that you are what you represent yourself to be?'

"'Yes, I can,' he answered, 'I can do this much—obtain the certificate of my father's and mother's marriage, and, after that, I can procure the certificate of my baptism; and I can bring friends who have visited my parents, and who usually saw me and looked upon me as one of the family, and no doubt was ever entertained of it.'

"'Well said: if you can do all this, you will be safe enough—the dangers of litigation cannot affect you. You will, I presume, have me commence legal proceedings at once against them, to obtain the rights and property they retain of yours.'

"'Exactly; I will give you the names and addresses of my brothers and sisters, and their attorney—at least I believe he is. You will use your own discretion as to what you may do. I will furnish you with all the proofs and papers as you may require of me."

"We had much further conversation which it is needless to relate; the sum of the whole is, I undertook the cause, and he confided it to me. I received of him a sum of money which I named, to secure myself from loss, and agreed that I would communicate the next day, as being the most courteous and usual manner of procedure. I thought over the whole affair after my new client had left my chambers, and had the gratifying reflection that I had a good case to begin with—for this I always called my first case, for it was one of some importance, for the property alone that was coming to my client would be many thousand pounds, and the costs would be heavy.

" There was a prospect of this suit making some noise in the profession, and would, doubtless, draw some attention to me as the conductor—indeed, I had so many thoughts and hopes about this suit, that I shall not be able to tell you half the speculations it gave rise to in my own mind; however, next day I wrote to the solicitor of the family, whose name had been furnished me, and inquired if he acted for them in a professional capacity, requesting he would inform me if he would undertake to appear in a suit for them.

"I also gave him a statement of the case—as much of it, at least, as I deemed necessary or expedient, demanding of them a restitution of all that had been seized upon for my client, and concluding with an intimation that proceedings would be forthwith commenced to enforce that which was withheld.

" In about a day's time I received a letter, intimating that they were the attorneys to the family, and would accept any process I might be instructed to issue out; and the following concluding paragraph of the letter exhibited to me the nature of their defence, which was as follows :—

" ' In answer to your demand, we have to inform you that your client has no claims upon the family, he not being one of the late Mr. Smirk's children by his wife, but merely one by some other person ; and having no children of their own in the early period of their marriage, they adopted him. After this they had children, but he was allowed by them to retain his position in the family— they thinking, no doubt, there would be ample time to settle family affairs, and to provide for him in a proper manner, without the necessity of formally disowning him.

" ' Thus, you see, has a claim arisen without any show of justice. If, after this, you still desire to prosecute the suit you say you are

instructed to commence, we are acting attorneys for the family, who
are determined to resist it. We will undertake to make an
appearance, or put in an answer to any bill you may file, or process
you may issue.'

"I read this letter over and over again, but I could not make out
anything that was very probable in all this. It is either true, I
thought, or not. In the first case it may be accounted for on the
principle that truth is stranger than fiction; and in the second, it
is too unlikely to make any good defence in a court of law.

"It was, I thought, a possible thing, yet by no means a probable
one. Had he been some foundling, the matter might have been
more likely; but an illegitimate child of the husband, to be received
into the family by the wife, and that, too, where there were children
of her own who would be seriously injured by it—it was too monstrous, I thought, to be any way near true, and my client must
win the day.

"I need hardly say I wrote to Mr. Smirk, enclosing him a copy
of the letter, and received from him an intimation that that was
the tale he himself had heard before, and it had made no impression
upon him; but he desired me to proceed with all possible despatch,
and to urge the matter on with such haste as the law would permit
me; as, while it was pending, he would be unable to pay attention
to anything—it would so far unhinge his mind that he could follow
no occupation with credit, and would therefore attempt none.

" Of course I was anxious about my case. I pushed it on with
what despatch I could, consistent with the character of a respectable
practitioner, which, · by the way, is not always at the rate that a
client desires; and it is difficult at all times to induce a belief in
the necessity of delay in proceedings connected with the administration of the law. They are, however, often needful and salutary,
and prevent the unfortunate defendant from being delivered into
the merciless hands of an enraged creditor. The suit went on
without any great impediment from the opposite party, who, in
fact, appeared anxious that an adjudication should be come to, and
the matter settled: they appeared to me to act confidently.

" Before the day of trial commenced, I had a lengthened interview with my client, Mr. Robert Smirk, and in that interview I learned nothing that shook my belief in the justice of his cause. He gave me the certificates, properly authenticated, of his father's marriage, and then of his own baptism at the same church, about three years after that marriage. This was plain enough—what more could I have or desire? and he showed me also copies of the certificates of his brothers and sisters, the eldest of whom was full two years younger than he.

" ' Well,' I said, ' all you have to do now, is to furnish proof of identity. Prove that you are the person whom the certificates apply to, and then there can be no further difficulty to contend with. You have friends whom you can bring to prove all that, who were well acquainted with your family ?'

" ' Yes, at least a score or two,' he replied, ' a score or two. I am confident in the truth and justice of my cause; but of course you look at this with a professional eye, and must have your doubts, not of the truth of what I have told you, but of the possibility of some hitch in the business, either in the affair itself, or in something turning up that was not known before. But, as far as I can see, there is nothing of that kind, and, therefore, I am confident; and a short time will now, I hope, restore to me the property of my father.'

" ' I hope so, too,' I replied, ' and, considering the proof you have furnished me with, and forming my opinion upon the facts of the case as they come under my own eyes, and not from what you have told me, I am quite confident of a victory. In any case, all they can do is to attempt to prove you illegitimate, which, with these certificates, I cannot but deem impossible—what kind of proof I cannot at all imagine—it is utterly beyond my powers of thought, because all is so plain. Have you any notion what is their line of action? Do you know what they will attempt, and how they will attempt it ?'

" ' I know of nothing more than this,—that when my mother died, I was not present. She declared to them, but enjoined secresy, that I was not her son, but an illegitimate son of my father's.'

" ' And have you any idea of the truth of that assertion?'

" ' None at all; I am quite sure that she made no such declaration. It is only a part of that malice with which they have treated me. I am convinced that nothing of the kind was ever said; and they can have none but suborned witnesses to aid them in such a course, and they can have but little moral weight against the respectable witnesses which I can produce on my behalf.'

" Well, thought I, there can be no difficulty in this matter, and yet the solicitors of the opposite side were really respectable men, who never would advise a suit so futile and so vexatious as this: they would not lend themselves to make a defence to such a cause, and thereby eat up the property of the children.

" This gave me a little food for thought, because I felt convinced that my opponents were confident of their cause, or, at least, they had a reasonable expectation that they would prove successful, else they would advise them to submit to some arrangement, an attempt to do which they had not made. If this were the case, where did their confidence arise?—it must have some cause; and what that was decidedly puzzled me. The more I thought of it, the more I was lost in conjecture.

" I had some calls from witnesses who were to be examined in this affair, but I could not at all find anything that threw any doubt on the matter. They all confirmed the view my own client took in the case, and that was, of course, most favourable to his success; and from them I learned that Mr. Smirk and his wife were very retired and quiet people, living much within themselves, and that for the first few years of their marriage they all travelled about from place to place for the benefit of Mrs. Smirk's health, who was at that time peculiarly delicate.

" Well, it matters not me, I thought; I have done my duty to my client, and I wish him success. I have done all my duty requires, and I must say that it will be a very interesting cause— one that will give them some little trouble in court; I shall expect to see it take some days. It will either be a good one or a complete failure.

" Thus were my thoughts occupied as the day of struggle

approached, and my excitement was naturally wound up to the greatest pitch by the scene that presented itself, in a long array of witnesses, counsellors with long flowing wigs, blue bags, and large briefs. I had several consultations with the barristers, and there were several of them, and they all examined the witnesses, so as to ascertain their exact position—so, in fact, they should be fully armed against all that could happen.

"Thus prepared, we entered court, and the business of the day was begun; for our cause was called on early, as it was expected that it would last several days, and, from the number of witnesses, and the length of counsels' speeches, would occupy a great deal of time; the fact being that the opening speech of counsel on one side, with the examination of our own witnesses, would at least take a day, if not a day and a half; and what time the adverse party might occupy, Heaven alone knew. I only thought that it was somewhat fortunate I had so much leisure to attend to the case, and give so much time to the development of the various matters connected with it, and to give a due idea of it to counsel, for I had bestowed much labour both upon the briefs and upon the consultations that had been had.

"The first day passed well enough. The opening speech was capital. I considered my client a very fortunate man, to think he had such an attorney, such a case, and such counsellors: he might be sure of victory. The certificates were put in and read, and there was no attempt made to impugn them, but they were coldly looked upon by the contending counsel, one of whom pointed at them, and, lifting his eyebrows, made some remark to one of his brethren in the cause, but nothing more passed.

"Then some of my witnesses were examined. They deposed to their knowledge of the parties; that they had known the parties for more than thirty years, and had been in the habit of visiting them, and had always considered Mr. Robert Smirk as the son of the deceased lady and gentleman. He was always introduced to strangers as their eldest son; they had visited them at various times, and never saw any difference between the claimant and the other children; there were none who ever saw any difference made, or any remark uttered, as far as they knew, and he was always treated with great affection.

"On their cross-examination, they admitted they had not been present at the birth, nor had they seen the child until after he had been weaned; that Mrs. Smirk had delicate health, and travelled about much in the company of her husband, and they only saw them at intervals. They were not at the christening, and they did not know who was the sponsors. They were not at all aware of the auspicious event before the child came home from nurse. They did not know anything about it, in fact, until the child appeared, ready made, as the counsel termed it, among them. All they knew was, there was a child, and that they believed him to be the son of the deceased Mr. and Mrs. Smirk.

"So far all was satisfactory, and thus the first day ended. I was in an ecstasy. My client's case, even after a lengthened cross-examination, had come out of that ordeal, even looking at it coldly, in a manner that gave me the greatest hopes of success.

"There appeared, however, a formidable array of talent against us, and I once or twice trembled; but then I remembered that I had a good cause, and I had good counsel—men of business, tact, and talent, who were fully equal to what had been arrayed against us; but still, as there was every disposition to contest my point, and fight the battle inch by inch, I could not but weigh every word that was drawn from the witnesses, to ascertain what unfavourable construction could be put upon their words; but I could see nothing unfavourable at all. They had elicited a few negatives, yet a host of negatives will never make an affirmative, and as those they had drawn contradicted nothing that had been said by our counsel, so nothing had been gained by them.

"The next day came, and the cause was resumed.

"There was much animation, and a great show of grey, curly heads, white faces, and black gowns, as well as other strangers. The examination of witnesses was continued; about fifteen or sixteen witnesses were examined, and all of them deposed to the same facts, and to about the same degree of utility, as that which I have already related. They were intimate with the family, and

all declared they believed Mr. Robert Smirk to be the eldest son
of his father, and that, being born after marriage, they believed him
legitimate—a very reasonable and probable deduction indeed,
and one in which I thought everybody must concur.

"Our case closed, and there was an adjournment for an hour, to
give the court time to refresh itself and the jury, which, as one of
our counsel said, was very seasonable to our adversaries, who
would employ the interval in consulting on the best means, and
the best line of defence; but it mattered not, they said, for they
could not see what defence they had to such an action : it was as
yet clear, but we must wait.

"The hour expired, and the counsel were in readiness, and when
the judge returned to his seat, the counsel for the defence rose to
reply. It was an elaborate and excellent speech, I must admit,
and I listened to it with profound interest and attention.

"He began by endeavouring to dissipate the effects of the eloquence of his learned friends who had gone before him, and wished
them—the jury—simply to look at the case as one of dispute between two parties, to one of whom they must give fortune by their
verdict; but in the formation of their opinion, he trusted they would
only be influenced by the weight and extent of the evidence.

"He then went on to say, that Mr. and Mrs. Smirk had been
married early in life. Their marriage had not sprung from any
lengthened courtship, but had been one that had been made by their
parents, and not sought by the parties themselves, and yet, unlike
most such marriages, it had turned out a very happy one, especially
on the lady's part, who was virtuous and amiable. But to their
sorrow they had during the earlier part of their marriage no
children, for whom they passionately longed. They desired the
blessings that others had bestowed upon them with so profuse a
hand, but of which they were themselves denied any participation.

"'Whatever might have been the original cause,' said the learned
counsel, 'I cannot now tell; but this is certain, a *liaison* sprung
up between the late Mr. Smirk and a beautiful young female, of
the name of Janson.'

"'Now, gentlemen,' said the barrister, 'you are all aware that the private life of individuals present, many events which are better left to slumber on in their obscurity and not to be raked up as it were from the ashes of the dead ; but under some circumstances it is necessary to institute an inquiry which call to light the obsolete acts of a deceased man's past life, and to make these painfully evident, and to prove them, and that which we shall be compelled to prove to-day, my lord, is not done with any desire to cast a slur on the deceased gentleman, far from it, but it is our duty to do what we are about to do.

" ' Elizabeth Janson, whom we shall prove is the mother of the claimant Robert Smirk, was the waiting-maid who was employed to attend upon Mrs. Smirk. She was her personal attendant, and travelled about with her and her master wherever they went.

" ' Two years had passed since their marriage, and yet there was no promise of children ; and for these they pined. About that time, or soon after, Elizabeth Janson left the service of Mrs. Smirk, and retired, no doubt for the purpose of hiding her shame, to live under the protection of her mother, with whom she remained until after the birth of Robert Smirk, who now claims to be the legitimate son of his father, by another mother.

" ' With some ulterior object, which it would be useless now to speculate upon,' continued the counsel, ' Mr. Smirk caused and permitted Elizabeth Janson and her illegitimate child to go to the same church where he was married, and there in his own presence, as appears from the signature in the register, had the child christened in the name of Robert Smirk, his own name, and as his own legitimate child. We have proof of this, gentlemen, and this is one point which I would wish to impress upon your minds, and that you'll remember is a point, too, which I shall be able to prove by respectable testimony.

" ' This *liaison* between Mr. Smirk and Elizabeth Janson was, however, of short continuance afterwards, for some officious person having witnessed the ceremony of christening, informed Mrs. Smirk of it, and the natural consequences were an *eclaircissement*, which took place.

" ' As I have before said, Mrs. Smirk was a very amiable woman, and she overlooked her husband's fault, and agreed to receive the child in her own house, upon condition that the young woman would leave the country in some family; but she would not live with her husband, or do anything for the child, if that condition was not complied with.

"'It is needless to say the condition was gladly submitted to, and the child was reared by Mrs. Smirk, who evinced in a short time a decided affection for the child, and it was educated and introduced to friends as her own child.

"'Elizabeth Janson was sent to India as an attendant upon a lady and family, and a small pension given her, provided she remained there, but it would cease if she returned, and it would be for her child's benefit that she should do so.

"'Two years after this, Mrs. Smirk herself was blessed with a child of her own—a son.

"'She had ever desired to have children, and now her wish was gratified; but this made little or no alteration in the situation of Robert Smirk, who retained his position; for he had gained the lady's affections so much that the presence of her own child caused no diminution in those feelings of regard and affection, but he was allowed to retain his position until her death: when on her death-bed, she summoned her children, and declared to them the secret, and enjoined them that they should keep it secret as long a their father lived, and to make no use of it even then, unless they were about to be deprived of all by him.

"'The time has come, gentlemen of the jury, when it is necessary that the secret should be divulged, and it is divulged. The only witnesses produced are those who merely depose to what I have now told you; but I shall produce those, whose testimony cannot be doubted, who will tell you all they have told you, and more. All that I have told you. We do not impute any intentional attempt to defraud on the part of the claimant; we believe he thinks he is the person whom he states himself to be; but, my lord and gentlemen, we can produce in court his *mother!*'

"Here was a fix. We, that is, attorney, counsel, and claimant, all looked at each other in amazement, but there was no time to think, for the witnesses were called to support, by their testimony, the case as made out by the counsel.

"The first witness who was called was the clerk of the church before whom the christening took place; and he deposed to the lady who attended as mother with the infant, was not the same Mr. Smirk had been married to but three years before, but declared he should recollect the lady at any time: she was remarkably beautiful, but had a long scar across the back of her hand. He recognised the person in court, and the scar was present, though he declared the lady greatly altered.

"The mother of Robert Smirk was called. She was a middle-aged woman, who, even now, possessed great personal attractions. She declared she was the mother of a child by Mr. Smirk, and that it was baptized in the manner described, and related all the circumstances that had been explained by the counsel; and she said she had not long returned from India, where she had married, and had now a large fortune. She was a widow with no children, and had returned to England, to live here, and to find out her child, whom she longed to see, and to bestow her fortune upon him; that she had gone to Mr. Smirk's family, to ascertain if he were alive but had found that his father was dead, and, calling upon his solicitors, she was subpœnaed as a witness. She only now came forward more to claim her son than to give testimony, for the fortune in dispute was nothing to what she herself possessed.

"There was another matter of astonishment; she was but slightly cross-examined, but nothing was elicited, and there appeared nothing more to say or do. The counsel all reposed in their enormous wigs, and listened to his lordship's address, which was lengthy; and, when that was ended, it was decided that my client was not the person he always thought himself to be, but somebody else. I lost my cause; but, thanks to good fortune, I gained my cause, and my client had nothing to bewail, for he had a much more ample fortune given him by his real mother, who was delighted to find such a son after so long an absence."

"What do you think of that, sir?" said Gage, when he had finished.

Mr. Bootle made no reply: he had been fast asleep for the last quarter of an hour.

CHAPTER XVII.

THE CONSULTATION AT THE JARVISES.

Mr. BLOOMENBACK had taken the extraordinary step of calling upon Mr. Gage in the manner he had done, quite unknown to the Jarvises; for he considered—and justly enough, too—that his interest in the whole of the transaction was quite as great as theirs; and, when we come to consider that he had fully made up his mind to share the spoil with them, we cannot feel surprised that he should take the initiative in any affair which he considered would advance his objects; and, as we know he was not very particular, provided he did achieve a result, how he achieved it, we may very well give him credit for the ingenious manner in which he sought to throw the onus of proving the legitimacy of Marianna upon Mr. Gage.

Of course that gentleman could not quarrel with the result of anything that he set about proving himself.

"And what a goose he must be," chuckled Mr. Bloomenback to himself; "what a goose he must be, to be sure, not to perceive that it's to the illegitimate, base-born Marianna Bootle that the money is left, and not to Marianna Brotherton. And if he do perceive it and heed it not, the man is certainly a greater donkey than I could have believed him capable of being, to sacrifice for a mere empty sound a princely fortune. Truly there is no accounting for tastes."

Having thus, as he considered, secured the co-operation of Mr. Gage in the great affair by which the payment of the legacy was

to be avoided, Mr. Bloomenback, with all the smirking appearance of self-satisfaction that can be imagined, took his way on
the following morning to the Jarvises.

Truly there was something awfully malicious in the character
of this man, or he could not have chuckled to himself as he did at
the prospect of the bitter disappointment which Selina and her
brother Hannibal would experience when they found out to what
a couple of adventurers they had united themselves.

Mr. Bloomenback must have been a very demon of mischief, for
what real good could it do to him that Selina and her brother should
be so frightfully deceived ?

He looked upon it, however, as a little pleasant after-piece—as
a something not belonging to the action of the real drama—but
still a little matter which formed a part of the general amusement.
It was a something to make him laugh in the midst of graver
concerns—a little piece of quiet malice which did not interfere at
all with his general views, but came across him in the shape of a
mental relaxation in his pleasanter moments.

"I only hope," he muttered to himself, as he reached the door-
step of the Jarvises, in Park Lane, "I only hope that I may
have the opportunity of being present when the *eclaircissement*
takes place—that will be a glorious treat. I fancy I see
poor, fast Hannibal with his bargain, and the charming Selina
with hers—the idiots—idiots both of them—they deserve all
they get; and now to reap some of the reward of my own ingenuity is, at all events, an acknowledgement of it from Rhododendron Jarvis."

Mr. Jarvis was of course at home to Mr. Bloomenback; and,
indeed, he had been up so late over-night that, although then the
morning was tolerably advanced, he had not been long seated in
the breakfast-room.

He had brought down with him from his chamber the pleasant
accompaniment of a sick head-ache. Hannibal did not show himself at all, but the fair Selina did appear at the breakfast, although
considerably the worse from the overnight's proceedings.

The self-satisfied air with which Mr. Bloomenback sat himself down was sufficient to convince the Jarvises that he considered everything was in a very pleasant state.

If he abstained from at once communicating all that had passed, it was not on account of the presence of Miss Jarvis and her mother, for Rhododendron Jarvis had made no secret to his family of the nefarious proceedings by which he had induced old Bootle to believe the dishonour of his child.

If they did not know the exact particulars, they knew that they owed their fortune to some chicanery, which they were quite willing to wink at, on account of its glittering results.

As Selina herself remarked, more than once, people need not be very particular now-a-days how they made money, so long as they did make it; and thus we may conclude that Mr. Bloomenback need not, by any means, have been particular in what he said before her; but then the breakfast-room, which was continually open to the presence of servants, was not the proper place in which to enter into a conference.

Mr. Jarvis, therefore, when the meal was concluded, led the way into his library—his library—the library of a man who never opened a book, and who thought every branch of literature quite beneath the attention of a man of the world, such as he was; but the house-agent had told him that room was the library, and, therefore, the library it remained.

"You seem pleased," he said to Bloomenback, "but last night's dancing, and drinking, and worrying have regularly upset me; have you got anything fresh to tell me?"

"I have, Jarvis: ever watchful as I am, of your interests, I have got to tell you that I have actually persuaded Gage himself to take the greatest pains, and feel the utmost interest, in proving the marriage of Lucinda Bootle."

"How did you manage that? does he not know that with that proof the legacy vanishes?"

"He must know it; as a professional man, he cannot but know it; the terms of the codicil are quite precise. You have but to hold the legacy, asking for Marianna Bootle to be produced— there's no such person; the child's name is Marianna Brotherton;

she does not answer the description of the legatee; and, although the Chancellor, if his court was put in motion about the matter, might say he regretted it, he would afford her no relief."

"You think we are safe, then, against a suit in equity?"

"Unquestionably; no chancery lawyer would lay down the dangerous precedent that a legacy was to be handed over to an individual misnamed and misdescribed in the will, because it appeared that he or she appeared to be the person meant by the testator."

"I understand that; but how did you bring Mr. Gage into your way of thinking?"

"By promising him a thousand pounds."

"What! another thousand pounds?"

"Yes, only two more, and then you save, you know, ten thousand five hundred pounds—a fortune in itself."

"Yes, but I thought you said you had promised him only a thousand pounds?"

"True, but you forget another thousand for myself, and I appeal to you if it be not dirt cheap, under the circumstances, to get Mr. Gage's concurrence in what we are about for two thousand pounds?"

"It seems to me, Bloomenback," said Jarvis, in a vexed tone, "as if you were determined to have it all by degrees."

"Stuff—nonsense! I'm pulling you through it; and now let me tell you, Jarvis, that we cannot too soon prove the marriage of Lucinda Bootle to Lieutenant Brotherton. You know how we succeeded in disproving it, or rather in so arranging circumstances that she could not prove it, or any one in her behalf."

"I know," said Jarvis, "that you seem to have made a cat's-paw of me throughout this business. It was you, Cousin Bloomenback, who first mooted the matter, stating that you had accidentally discovered the secret marriage of Lucinda Bootle, and how you knew it would enrage her father."

"Well!"

"You then stated that you knew of circumstances that would enable you, with my co-operation, to make it appear she was the mistress and not the wife of Lieutenant Brotherton, and consequently to shut the door against reconciliation between the father and daughter for ever."

"Very well," said Mr. Bloomenback; "since we are making out a catalogue of what we have done, allow me to state that it was you who went with me to St. John's Chapel, near Totteridge, broke into the sacred edifice at night, and took the leaf out of the registry, that contained the entry of the marriage of Lucinda Bootle with Alexander Brotherton."

"Hush! hush! no more of this!"

"Nay, let's have it all out. We went again with another leaf so accurately like the one we had abstracted from the registry, with every name accurately entered on it but those we wished to suppress, and that forged leaf, I own, I so accurately inserted in the volume that nothing appeared to be missing."

"Yes; you did it, you did it, you know."

"I know I did it, while you stood by holding me a light while your coward hands trembled so, that the flickering glare was of little use to me."

"And then, and then—you it was who bribed a servant at Devizes to steal the certificate which Mrs. Brotherton had of her union."

"I did, and it was cleverly done; so that the parson being dead who married them, and the old clerk likewise, who gave the bride away, there was not a tittle of evidence to be had of the marriage if any one had given a million of money for it. Was it not well managed? Could anything be better? And now you grudge me the necessary payment for my labour. On my life, I ought to charge you double what I do!"

"I'm sure," said Jarvis, as he wiped the damp perspiration from his brow, "I'm sure I did not begin this recrimination. The thing has answered its purpose; and now you say the marriage is to be proved to save this twenty-five thousand pounds. How is that to be done, when we have ourselves destroyed all the evidence?"

G

"I beg your pardon," said Bloomenback, "I never destroy anything. I have
the certificate of the marriage. I have the
leaf that was torn out of the registry."

"You have them? Impossible! Why,
I saw you cast them into the flames with
my own eyes."

"You saw me cast into the flames a bit
of parchment and a bit of paper similar in
size and shape to those documents; but I

kept the original, Mr. Jarvis. I thought they might be useful some day. I have several times wondered what old Mr. Bootle would give for them."

" Gracious heavens! Have I for years stood upon the brink of such a precipice?"

" That's just where you have stood; and now understand me—I will have half. Jarvis, do you hear that? I will have half. For every shilling you get, I will demand, and I will have, sixpence If your income be fifteen thousand pounds per annum, it shall be divided by two, and I will have half of it. I will have it signed, sealed, delivered, and made over to me in the strongest possible manner that the law can compass; now you understand all that, Mr. Jarvis, and we need have no further exclamations between us."

" You villain!" said Jarvis.

" You scoundrel!" cried Bloomenback.

" Do you not dread that you will drive me to an extremity, and that I may expose all, and so effect your destruction, even if I compass my own?"

" Not at all," said the lawyer, " you're too great a coward; I've no fears of the sort, but you may have as many as you please. The question you will have to ask yourself is, whether you will have half old Bootle's fortune, letting me have the other half, or nothing? I am pretty comfortably off; you are a ruined man. I have some relations in America, from which secure haven I can denounce you quietly and comfortably."

" No, no, no! Do as you please, Bloomenback, but let us—let us hang together."

" Hang! Did you mean hang?"

" No, no! Hush, hush! the word slipped out by chance. Do what you like, manage as you will, I am completely in your hands."

" Very good," said the lawyer, " that's sensible; and now I shall set about proving the marriage. Good day, Jarvis, you don't somehow or another look quite comfortable."

CHAPTER XVIII.

RETRIBUTION.

MR. BLOOMENBACK was right. Jarvis did not look, somehow or another, quite comfortable; and when the lawyer was gone, and he was alone in that magnificent apartment, he shook like one in an ague, and a cold perspiration broke out upon every limb, while the sight he caught of his own haggard countenance, in a mirror that hung opposite to him, was absolutely terrifying.

"What is this? what is this?" he said, as he strove to reassure himself; "what strange terrors are these that creep over my soul? I never suffered like this when I was a struggling man with no fortune! I never shook in this way when several times my prospects have been ticklish enough! What comes over me now, when, at the worst, I am sure of a princely income? What a fool I am to shake in this way! I suppose now some people would call this retribution."

He started as he heard the handle of the door turned, and, with a half scream, he cried,—

"No, no! Take Bloomenback—take Bloomenback—not me, not me!"

"Sir," said a footman, entering the apartment, "my mistress wishes to know when you require the carriage?"

"Oh! yes—yes—yes! I was only acting—acting a little; we—we—think of having some private theatricals, and what you overheard me speak was a mere speech."

"If you please, sir—yes, sir."

"So, so, you take no notice of it?"

"Oh dear no sir! of course not, sir."

"You are prudent—you are prudent! Tell your mistress I will drive out now."

"Yes, sir—certainly, sir."

Mr. Jarvis did drive out; but the haggard expression of his face, and the general appearance of mental suffering that was about him, could not have escaped the observation of the most superficial observer. Mrs. Jarvis, of course, noticed it, and asked the question, which he evaded, ascribing what he felt to the score of indisposition consequent upon the last night's late hours ; and as the lady did not feel very well herself from the same cause, the excuse to her assumed a very valid shape.

It is true that the carriage was driven round all the fashionable districts—it is true that the gorgeous and blazoned panels attracted much remark, and that the silver mounted harness flashed in the eyes of many a longing pedestrian, who fancied that the possessor of so much glory and magnificence could not, by any possibility, be other than a very happy man indeed.

And this is the way the heedless crowd speculate upon the fortunes of others ; this is the way that those who might and ought to be contented when they can look into their breasts and find there no cankering care, envy those who are, perhaps, doomed not to know a moment's peace, and who are, like slaves with gilded chains, making a part of the gorgeous pageant of some great conqueror, but being themselves so sick at heart that they could lie down by the wayside and die from very grief and shame.

If Mr. Jarvis had asked himself the question, he would have owned, had he been induced to tell himself the truth, that, after the first flush of excitement and pleasure consequent upon believing himself the possessor of so much wealth, he had not known a moment's peace.

But then the source from which he had obtained it was a limited one, and he began to doubt an axiom that was very current in his family—an axiom which we have heard Miss Selina quote, and in the truth of which they all firmly believed, which was, " that it was no matter how you got money, so long as you did get it."

Mr. Jarvis had money, and yet he was wretched.

He was very glad when the drive was over ; and, when he got home again, he was more glad still that it was a time of day which gave him an excuse for dipping deeply into a wine-bottle by way of luncheon.

That restored him a little ; and when, likewise, several visitors dropped in, and he began to feel a little better, in consequence of the action of the stimulant, he had hopes, after all, of achieving some of the results which he had pictured to his imagination in his happiest moods.

And so the day wore on, Mr. Jarvis finding that whenever he got very uncomfortable the wine-cup restored him a little.

But what a life to lead, only quenching the agony of remorse in the strong action of vinous compounds; and how he dreaded, too, to go about his own house for fear he should meet Marianna! He did see her once upon the staircase that day, and he shrank back, like a guilty thing as he believed himself to be, and closed the door of his room till the young girl had passed.

He felt that he could not bear the glance of those large, melancholy-looking eyes; he knew that he was the traducer of the mother—he knew that he was the virtual destroyer of the father—he fancied that he knew that he sent old Mr. Bootle to the grave with sorrow, and how dared he, after that, look upon the face of any one so young and innocent as Marianna Brotherton?

But the young child was happier than he thought her; for, first of all, she was happier in that possession which he could never know again, that birthright with which all human nature starts, but which so many squander—a pure and uncorrupted heart.

She was happy, too, in the society of one whose friendship she relied upon, and who, notwithstanding all his peculiarities of manner, and his want of that high culture she had herself received, she soon learned to estimate—that one was no other than her friend Job Brick.

He certainly did, by dint of downright perseverance and doing just what he liked, whether the Jarvises liked it or not, contrive to make the situation of Marianna very tolerable.

For example, Job would walk into the kitchen just as the dinner was being dished for table, and seizing upon some roast fowl or other delicacy, would bear it off in triumph and place it before the young girl, with all the costly *et ceteras* he could lay his hand on.

To be sure, great complaints were made of Job by the servants; but the Jarvises, from some reason or another best known to themselves, dared not discharge him ; the fact is, Job knew some secrets connected with the whole of them—little scandalous domestic secrets, which he never intended to make any use of, but which it amused him very much to held *in terrorem* over them—especially since the arrival of Marianna, whom he evidently looked upon as something strange and wonderful, and quite out of the common order of beings ; for every word she said was to him perfection, and everything she did must of necessity be right.

There was something pleasant and deeply philosophical in all this—it seemed as if nature had intended that these two opposite, as it were, in manners, mind, and appearance, should meet, and that they should esteem and admire each other because they were such opposites.

But be this how it may, one thing is quite evident, and that is the fact that a deep and lasting friendship was formed in the uncongenial atmosphere of Rhododenderon Jarvis's house, between Marianna Brotherton and the simple, just, and high-minded Job Brick.

How trifling a circumstance will make things endurable, which otherwise would transcend all human patience ! It would have been next to impossible for Marianna to have remained at the Jarvises, had it not been for the kindly aid of Job ; for otherwise, if she had had the patience of Job's celebrated namesake, she must have turned against the insults that were hourly heaped upon her innocent head.

There is certainly a propensity in the human mind to persecute. Let the heads of a family but show that any one member is unconsidered, and that unfortunate member will become persecuted by the whole household. The Park Lane servants soon found out of how little consideration was poor, dependant Marianna.

The very footmen seemed to think that they might call the orphan, dependant girl by her Christian name, if they chose ; and if they met her on the staircase, there was not the smallest shadow of respect shown to that hapless one, whom they considered to be an outcast.

But the child bore all this with a wonderful serenity. If anything was said to her that she did not like the matter or the manner of, she simply contented herself by not answering it. But a kindly remark she was always ready, in as kindly a manner, to respond to, let it come from whom it might. It was rare indeed though, except from Job Brick, that she was put to that trouble.

One would have thought that Mrs. Jarvis must have felt some touch of womanly compassion for that poor, friendless girl; but she did not. Her heart was so warped by cold selfishness, that she never for one moment considered what must be the feelings of Marianna, cast as she was, poor thing! among strangers.

And yet this woman had been a mother! But, alas! the old proverb which insinuates so gracefully the difficulty of making a silken purse out of a sow's ear, forces its truthfulness upon us at every turn.

Mrs. Jarvis was a thoroughly selfish woman, and she was not educated enough to know that her best interests lay in concealing that predominating trait in her character.

And, strange as it may appear, we are inclined, of the whole family, to give Mr. Jarvis most credit for feeling towards Marianna. A man, let him be ever so selfish, or ever so criminal, never can wholly divest himself of some feelings of compassion for a young girl, and there were times when he did feel a touch of compunction.

Perhaps, if some such happy moment had been pounced upon by Mr. Gage, Jarvis might have consented to some rather liberal allowance for the orphan; but then, these fits of generosity soon passed away, and unhappily, when the affair was urged to him, he was, like King Richard,—

"Not i' the vein."

The attack upon his future prospects by Bloomenback now, however, occupied all his thoughts, to the exclusion of every other topic. It appeared to him to be so monstrous (and so it was,) that the lawyer should demand half, that the disquietude upon that score was far more energetic a feeling than any congratulations upon the ground of slipping into £7,500 per annum.

But thus it is ever with large affairs, as well as small, and with matters in which there is no iniquity, as well as in those for which humanity should blush. It is what is lost that is esteemed, and which successfully attacks the imagination, while that which is in possession soon loses the gloss which it assumed to the mind, when seen through the halo of the apparently unattainable distance.

The very demon of restlessness seemed to have taken possession of Mr. Jarvis. He could rest nowhere, and, after Bloomenback had left him, he rushed into the open streets, without carriage and without attendance, hoping that a long walk would, by the very fatigue it would induce, calm his perturbed spirits.

And now, the day is drawing toward its close, and it is time that we should think of wafting our readers to the old, aristocratic gardens of Kensington Palace, where the young people—Hannibal and the Lady Georgiana, the gallant colonel and Selina—had agreed to meet, in order to enjoy converse sweet, and to whisper to each other those soft and tender nothings, which, we suppose, from the commencement of the world, have made up the staple of lovers' discourses.

CHAPTER XIX.

THE MEETING AT KENSINGTON GARDENS.

It is seven o'clock, one hour before sunset, and the fashionable world have left Kensington Gardens, in order to proceed homewards for dinner, that being about the time at which tyrant Custom has dictated the king meal of the day shall be partaken of.

A few pedestrians are still wandering about the shady walks certainly, but then they are composed of such as have had the sense to subdivide their time better, and, having dined at a reasonable hour, are able to enjoy the many beauties of a sunset among magnificent trees, and in a spot which makes one think himself far away from the busy hum of town existence.

Each moment the shadows from the huge chesnut-trees, that abound in that pleasant locality, are stretching further across the glades and paths of the ancient garden.

The sun has caught some of the side windows of the palace, making them look like fretted gold, and the birds amid the branches of the tall trees are singing their orisons, ere they drop into deep slumber.

The Park is getting very thin of carriages, and the ride is nearly deserted, but from the Oxford-street gates enters a carriage. It is an open barouche, and in it are seated the hopes of the Jarvis family, in the shape of its male and female scions. Yes, Selina and Hannibal are going to keep their appointment, and, although the meeting was to have been just within the Bayswater-gate, they, as they had plenty of time, thought of entering the garden by the Park, and walking down the long path that runs parallel with the roadway, until they came to the gate named.

The barouche is a gaudy thing. It had been purchased by Mrs. Jarvis, and she had graciously lent it to the "children," as she affectionately, in her way, denominated Hannibal and Selina, not that she had any notion of the errand they were going upon, for, as is the case in all vulgar families, marriages in perspective were kept among the Jarvises quite quiet, instead of, as certainly ought to be the case, except as in some very special circumstances, being made as public as possible.

The brother and sister never had been so friendly and confiden-tial before in all their lives as they were now, for the general characteristics of the Jarvises had certainly been a sort of domestic wrangling, which was dreadfully at variance with that amiable feeling, which some benighted individuals, who know little of real life, suppose to exist in families.

The fact is, there is nothing in the world, in the shape of dis-like, that can come near a good old family hatred, founded upon a perfect knowledge of the parties, and which is as enduring as life itself.

We do not mean to say that the Jarvises ever got so far as that; but certainly we can say, that the good understanding between the

brother and sister now was something quite new, and would have
been wonderful, had it not been, as we happen to know, founded on
what they considered to be a mutuality of interests.

About the same time that the Jarvises got out of the showy
barouche at the entrance to Kensington Gardens from the Park, a
rather shabby cab drove up to the Bayswater-gate; and from the

rattling, dirty vehicle there alighted the Honourable Colonel
Mildmay and the Honourable Georgiana Damer. There was, of
course, the usual wrangle about what was to pay, and the usual

abuse, when only half as much again as the real fare was given, after which the two honourable personages smoothened their ruffled pinions, and entered the gardens.

It was scarcely to be expected that either party was to be punctual to a minute; but they did meet about half way along the broad path we have mentioned, and then what a shaking of hands ensued, and what a profusion of smiles bloomed upon every countenance! It is really delightful to think how pleasant human nature can be, when it likes.

But the quartette did not remain long together. Hannibal and the Honourable Georgiana took precedence, and walked for a time rather fast, while the gallant officer and Selina walked rather slow, the effect of which pleasant and delicate arrangement was, that the parties could meet again when they chose; but that in the meantime they did not at all interfere with each other, or disturb the sweet communion of souls that was taking place.

"And so," answered the colonel, in the most approved lack-a-daisical fashion, "and so, dear one, you have indeed come so far to bless me by your presence." (The amazing distance was from Park Lane.)

"I promised," said Selina, with an air and manner which seemed to imply that, having made a promise of any sort, she preferred keeping it, to the preservation even of her existence.

"Yes; and upon that promise I have existed, since last we met in the glittering halls. Oh Selina, never, until I looked upon you, did I know what it was to love."

"Men are such flatterers."

"Not all men. But Selina! oh, Selina! I have done a deed since last we met that surely must have been the frantic act of the moment. I have tossed all night upon a restless couch, till my nerves were all unstrung. I have done a deed which, if you should orgive, makes me the happiest of men; but if you should condemn, and cast me off for, I shall feel that a plunge into the quiet waters of yonder round pond can alone atone for."

"You terrify me."

"Oh, no—no; say not that."

" But you do. Oh, tell me what dreadful deed it was that you have done ?"

" I will, I must. But you will reproach me, Selina; you will fly from me. You will tell me that you hate me, and that you never, in all your young and beautiful existence, heard of the like."

The curiosity of Selina was wound up to the highest pitch, for she had not the smallest possible clue to what the colonel meant, and she was completely lost in a maze of hurried conjecture, as to what the deed could possibly be that he had done, and which was calculated to produce such diabolical effects: she knew that it would indeed be something wonderful and outrageous that would induce her to fly from him, whom she had thoroughly made up her mind to entangle in the noose matrimonial, if she possibly could.

No wonder, then, that she was in a perfect fever of impatience to know what the deed was that placed so pleasant and so determined upon a consummation in jeopardy.

" Speak," she exclaimed, " oh, dear, tell me all!"

" Oh, Heaven!" cried the colonel—" was that endearing epithet applied to me?—was it indeed?—did you call me by the name of dear?—oh, did you? Say so again!"

" You quite alarm me. What I want is, to know the deed you speak of. For Heaven's sake tell me what it is at once, or I intend to faint away."

" No, no—oh, no! My heart and brain are alike distracted. I have—put up the banns!"

" The—the banns of mat——"

" Rimony," concluded the colonel; " and now, like some poor prisoner, I await my sentence. Is it to be life and joy, or the round pond?"

What a weight was taken off Selina's heart! This was the dreadful deed,—it might turn out a dreadful one when he knew the temper he had to deal with, but it certainly was not at all dreadful to her, for the information fell like balm upon her soul, and she had to turn her head away to hide the expression of pleasure that sat upon her face, and which she thought it would be indiscreet of her to allow her lover to behold.

"You cast me off," he cried, " you cast me off for ever. Farewell! Now for the round pond!"

"No, no!" exclaimed Selina, catching him by the skirt of his coat, as he showed a disposition to be off at once, and carry his threat of plunging into the round pond into execution,—" no, no— oh, no!"

"What do I hear? Is it the voice of my Selina that bids me live?"

"Yes, yes, yes!"

"Oh joy!—oh rapture!—oh everything!"

"How could you really, colonel, be so precipitate as to put up the banns without consulting me? Oh, I ought really never look upon your deceiving face again; I ought to discard you. This is Tuesday, and then—then it is just possible that we might be married next Sunday."

"It is possible!—it is—oh, it is!" cried the colonel, with rapture. "Support me, ye heavenly powers! Sylvan nymphs and little lovers of all sorts, hold me in your arms! She will be mine! —she will consent, oh ye gods!—she will be Lady Mildmay, and cousin to two dukes, three earls, four viscounts, and half-a-dozen countesses next Monday! She will grace the court of the little queen—she will; her fair sparkling eyes say so."

" Oh, Mildmay, what power of eloquence you possess! You remind me of some great hero—it's all like a play."

"A play—a—a play—oh, a play—oh yes, very like a play."

From some reason or another, the gallant colonel did not seem at all to like the theatrical insinuation—it perhaps touched him on some tender point, so Selina did not press the simile; but after a little more pressing upon his part, she did graciously and whisperingly consent to be his, and say that it was necessary, as the policemen say, to move on, for the gates of the Gardens were about to be closed, and it was a great deal too romantic to be shut in there all night even with such a lover as the honourable colonel and such a companion as Lady Georgiana, his fair and aristocratic cousin.

We must not suppose that during all this time Hannibal Jarvis was idle—quite the contrary, for, to use his own most expressive phraseology, he was getting on like a house on fire. The lady managed him very nicely.

The moment the Honourable Georgiana, as Hannibal loved to call her, was alone with him, she took such a fit of trembling, that he got seriously alarmed, and in the most tender manner pressed her to disclose the cause of her evident great mental agitation. For a time she was obdurate, and resisted all his prayers and entreaties, but at length she said,—

"I must, I ought to tell you, that my cousin the colonel has done something which will separate us for ever, because it will lay me open to an imputation of forwardness, although I am completely innocent of it. Hannibal, we shall never meet again. This is the last time, dear Hannibal, I shall hear your voice."

"Oh, good gracious! don't say that. What has the colonel done? Oh tell me at once, unless you want to be the death of me! What has he done?"

The lady wept, and still said that it was cruel of the colonel, very cruel; and yet she did not tell the agonised Hannibal what it was, until at last, when he had become nearly frantic, and she saw that his impatience had indeed reached a most alarming height, she spoke more intelligibly.

"I must throw myself," she said, "entirely upon your personal faith in me to give me credit when I say that I am no party to what my cousin Mildmay has done, and which, however, I cannot help censuring him for, for I know it was done with the very best of motives. You could not guess, I am sure, were you to try for twelve months."

"Oh, don't torture me any more," said Hannibal, "but tell me what it is at once? I shall certainly fall down flat if you don't."

"Then—then—" faltered the Honourable Georgiana, and her tears flowed fast as she spoke—"then I have got to tell you that he has actually put up the banns of matrimony between himself and your sister Selina."

"Oh, is that all? I dare say Selina won't be very sorry.

What a relief it is, to be sure, to find that *that* is all you have to tell me!"

" Oh, I wish it was! What a dreadful state of feeling I am in! He did not do it for a joke; I can assure you he did not do it for a joke; but, as he tells me, an uncontrollable impulse came over him—an impulse that he could not shake off, and on the moment, certainly with little reflection, he—he actually ordered the banns to be published between you and I."

" What!" said Hannibal, with a shout, " and is that all? Oh, my eye! how pleased I am! Why—why, you didn't think that would cut me up, did you? Oh, Georgiana, if you only knew how I loved you! If you only knew how I have been thinking of you ever since I saw you, and how I haven't been able to take my victuals, you would pity me. Let me beg of you—it's rather damp, or else I'd go plump on my knees—but let me beg of you, beautiful Honourable Georgiana, as the banns are put up, not to let 'em be put up for nothing?"

" What can you mean? Oh, how my heart flutters! Hannibal, what do you mean?"

" Be mine, dear maid; be mine. Be Mrs.—no, I mean, be the Honourable Georgiana Jarvis! Do—oh, do!"

" What can I say? What can I do? Such devotion! Such chivalrous conduct! I—I—spare me, dear Hannibal,—I think— yes, I will be yours—yes, I will be Mrs. Jarvis."

CHAPTER XX.

AUNT SHUTER WORRIES THE JARVISES.

HAVING already accompanied Hannibal and his sister so far on the road to the hymeneal altar, we may safely now leave them to consummate what they consider their happiness, but which it seems highly probable will turn out, as Mrs. Jarvis would say, *vice versa.*

We must confess we are not particularly troubled at the generally bad aspect of the affairs of the Jarvises, for if ever people in this world deserved retribution they did, for the great evil they had done, and the still greater evil they contemplated.

If we could find any spark of kindly feeling among these Jarvises, we should regret to see them thus hurried on to such destruction. If Selina possessed any of those attributes of womanhood which lend to the female character its greatest charms, we should be sorry, indeed, to see her fall into the clutches of so heartless an individual as the self-styled Colonel Mildmay. And we should have a sigh of regret likewise ready for Hannibal, despite even all his folly, and all his desire to do the fast thing, if he had but uttered one word of pity or commiseration for the young girl, who had, by the force of wayward circumstances, been thrown upon him and his family for protection.

But in the whole career of the Jarvises, throughout the eventful transactions it has been our duty to record, have they exhibited one piece of feeling, which we can look back to with pleasure? Not one. For even the agony which Mr. Rhododendron Jarvis endured was rather that agony arising from disappointment than from any conscience-stricken feelings with regard to the morality of his deeds. He found himself uncomfortable, and therefore he regretted that which he had done, but not for the sake of the acts themselves; for if all had passed on smoothly and serenely with him, it would have been quite another affair, and he never would have heaved a sigh over those circumstances, which now he more than once most certainly wished had never taken place.

What was the splendour of his house to him if he were afraid, which he really was, of meeting the young girl upon the staircase? What enjoyment could he have of that capacious and costly mansion, if he slunk about it like a felon? And what was it to him that he had an income of seven thousand five hundred pounds per annum, if, instead of looking upon that as a matter of rejoicing, he only contrasted it with the similar amount he had lost, and made himself unhappy that he had not both?

Truly, Mr. Jarvis had not by any means advanced his temporal felicity by his achievements in the way of stealing marriage certificates, extracting leaves from church-registers, and defaming the fair fame of those who in excellence and virtue were as superior to him as angels of light are to destructive demons seeking whom they may devour.

The time hung most laggingly upon his hands; he knew not what to do with himself, and, notwithstanding all affairs looked so promising, as regarded the actual fact of his at all events becoming possessed of what, with all its deductions, would be a splendid fortune, he was uneasy.

Old commercial axioms of business kept thronging to his mind; he knew that there was many a slip betwixt the cup and the lip, and that, although the bowl of fortune seemed to be held up to him to quaff from, he was, Tantalus-like, forbidden to slake his thirst in the golden stream.

Oh, how he longed for Mr. Smith to come home from his continental tour! and whenever he thought of that individual, he pictured to himself a thousand dangers that might by possibility arise to the precious document of which he was the possessor.

What—if the will were lost! What—if some inn, in which Mr. Smith reposed his weary bones, was to catch fire, involving both Smith and will in a roaring conflagration! What—if the vessel in which he sought to cross the Channel were to sink, and the will lie five fathoms' deep beneath the salt sea wave! What—if Mr. Smith were to be attacked by robbers, by eccentric Italian banditti, who, perchance, for want of anything better for the purpose, might scorch Mr. Smith's whiskers off with that will which was of such importance to him—Jarvis!

These were not agreeable ideas; and although it was just possible that, had it come to the push, Mr. Rhododendron Jarvis might have proved himself heir-at-law, that was a point he was by no means quite certain of; he knew there had been a Mr. Bootle, who had gone abroad somewhere, a younger brother of old Jeremiah, and who was reported to have died, but he might not be dead for all that; so that Mr. Jarvis truly could have exclaimed,—"The will—the will's the thing!"

It was in this state of dreadful anxiety and doubt that a day or two passed away—a day or two of so much splendour and so much misery, that Mr. Jarvis very much doubted which predominated, for he was kept in a constant whirl between the two.

Bloomenback called upon him once or twice, and assumed such airs of mastery over him and of undue importance, that if he, Jarvis, at some moments, had had a deadly weapon in his hand, the lawyer's life would have been worth but little.

Mr. Bloomenback, however, took things very coolly and pleasantly; he talked to Rhododenderon Jarvis as if they were the best friends in the world, and actually showed him the certificate of Lucinda's marriage, to assure him of the fact that those documents were still in existence, which he, Jarvis, had fondly believed were long since destroyed, and then, in the midst of all this, Mr. Gage dropped him a note to say that Mrs. Shuter had come to London, and was extremely anxious to call upon him for the purpose of seeing Marianna; the note added that the old lady did not know when she would call, but that it might be the next day, or possibly the day after, and Mr. Gage himself put in a postscript that she was so deaf that she always carried with her a slate and pencil, by means of which she carried on conversation.

Most gladly would Jarvis have foregone the pleasure of the visit, but Bloomenback urged him to put up with it, saying,—

"Your policy at present is to be upon good terms with everybody; if you don't know what a protracted will-case in the courts of law is, I do. The slightest opposition may throw all this affair into Chancery, and Heaven only knows then what might be the result! At all events, it's far better to be civil to a deaf old woman, and to tolerate the presence of Marianna, than to get involved in anything of the sort. I have myself quite a sufficient interest in the affair to advise that all law proceedings be kept out of."

Thus, then, was it that Jarvis was forced to prepare himself, as best he could, for the projected visit of Mrs. Shuter.

"It's one comfort," he said to his wife, "that she's so horribly deaf, she won't hear a word we say to her or of her, which is of more importance."

But the promised visit was delayed; and a day or two still elapsed before Mrs. Shuter made her gracious appearance in Park Lane; when she did, however, the Jarvises were taken most uncomfortably by surprise, for they had just got about half through a late breakfast, when Job Brick, with quite a delightful expression of countenance, flung open the door, and announced Mrs. Shuter.

"The devil!" said Jarvis.

"La, pa!" said Selina, "she'll hear you; Mr. Bloomenback says she's very rich, but that if she gets offended she'll cut us all off with   shilling."

"You need be under no apprehension," said Jarvis, "she's as deaf as a post, and they tell me she wouldn't hear a cannon-shot if it were fired close to her ears."

Enveloped in a collection of shawls and cloaks, that the old lady looked like a moveable wardrobe, she walked into the breakfast parlour of the Jarvises.

"Well, well," she said, as if addressing her servant, although that individual had not come further than the hall, "well, well, you can tell the coachman to call in an hour. I hear you—you think I am deaf because I carry a slate, but that's my fancy."

"How do you do, madam?" roared Jarvis in her ear.

"Yes, that's my fancy, and so people say I'm deaf."

"She don't hear a word you say, pa," said Selina.

"Well, then," remarked Jarvis, "you're a pretty good hand at a scream; ask her to take a chair, and if she don't hear you she'll hear nobody."

"Will you," shouted Selina, raising herself upon her tip-toes to reach Mrs. Shuter's ear, "will you take a chair?"

"My gracious! you'll split the drum of my ear," said Mrs. Jarvis; "for Heaven's sake, Selina, don't make that dreadful noise."

"Ah!" said Mrs. Shuter, "you've a quiet, respectable family, I dare say; but none of you have said anything yet. How do you all feel? It's a fine day—a very fine day, though my coachman thinks it will rain. Ah! well—perhaps it may. I'm Mr. Bootle's aunt; I told him I didn't want his property—what's his property to me? I've got plenty of property of my own. Let me see—it's my fancy—I aint deaf a bit—but it's my fancy, when anybody says anything to me, that they shall write it down on a slate."

With that she handed to Mr. Jarvis a slate and pencil that were dangling at her side, and he wrote upon it in large letters, " How do you do, Mrs. Shuter? I hope you are very well?" to which, after reading, she wrote the reply, " What's that to you?" Then Miss Selina wrote upon the slate, " That of course they felt interested in Mrs. Shuter's health, having heard that she was so good and amiable to the poor;" upon which Mrs. Shuter wrote a reply of—" It's all a lie, and you know it."

After this, as may be well supposed, the conversation flagged a little, and Mrs. Shuter took it up orally, having it, of course, all her own way.

" Yes, yes," she said, " people want to make out that I'm dead, and won't live long because I'm deaf. I dare say they'd like to cut me up. Yes, yes, I've got as much money to leave as Jeremiah Bootle any day; so what do I want with his property? I didn't want his property—what's his property to me? What I want to see, though, is if this child—this Marianna—is like the family, that's what I want to see; and if she is, I—I think I'll leave her three hundred thousand pounds Three per Cents., and to anybody who has said a kindly word to her, I'll pay them fifty pounds a piece; to anybody who has said, ' God bless her!' that's a hundred and fifty down. If she's like the family, and if she wept, and there was a kindly hand that stanched one of the tears, they shall have bank-notes in heaps—yes, in heaps, if she's like the family. What do I want with old Bootle's property—what's old Bootle's property to me? It's the family I look to."

" Do you hear her?" said Jarvis. " Was there ever such a mad woman in all this world?"

" I think she's a damned old fool," said Hannibal, who had come into the room during the colloquy.

" A shocking old frump!" cried Selina.

" She ought to be smothered," said Mrs. Jarvis. " I've no

patience with her; but we must do the best we can to get some of her money out of her."

This was a sentiment in which they were all perfectly agreed, and the old woman ran on talking without in the least noticing the injurious things that were said of her.

"Yes, yes, what do I want with his property? I want to know if she's like the family."

At this juncture Mr. Jarvis seized the slate, and wrote upon it the following words, which he thought would be a settler for Marianna :—

"My dear madam, you forget that the child you speak of is a b——d."

"A blasted what?" said the old woman. "How dare you speak of any one belonging to the family in such a way? I'll cut you all off with a fourpenny piece. Yes, yes, the man that cut off his own heir with a shilling shall be a fool to me. I'll cut you all off. Don't let me have any more swearing about the family; it's very wrong, and I won't bear it—the idea of writing such a word upon any female's slate, and the mock modesty, too, of writing it with a dash and *d* at the end of it. I'll cut all off with one of the new farthings that Joseph Hume invented to pay the twopenny omnibuses with and his own instalments on the Greek Loan. Yes, yes, I want to see if Marianna's like the family."

"Now was there ever," said Jarvis, "such a confounded old brute as this! I'll try her again, though."

He seized hold of the slate and wrote upon it in large characters, "You are very good, my dear madam, but Marianna is amply provided for by us—she is not like the family, and she is illegitimate; you had better not see her by any means."

"Oh, ah!" said the old lady, "you're another."

"What the devil does she mean," said Jarvis, "by I'm another? she's out of her wits, that's quite clear—the idea, now, of an old devil like this having money to leave."

"It's a blessed rummy go," said Job Brick, who had remained in the room all the while: "I never saw such a lark in all my life—my eye, what a topper she gave me with that ere slate as we was a coming up the stairs."

"I want to see the young girl," cried Mrs. Shuter, "I want to see if she's like the family—somebody fetch her directly, or else I'll cut you all off—I'll cut everybody off, and leave all my money to the Royal-Patent-General and Particular-Evangelic al-Visiting Anti-Parochial Society."

"Good God!" said Jarvis, "was there ever such an abominable society as that?"

Job Brick vanished, and in a few moments brought in Marianna Brotherton. The young girl glided into the room like a spirit of beauty, and as she approached, the Jarvises could not help noticing that old Mrs. Shuter's hands shook as though she had been palsied, and the slate dropped from her nerveless grasp. Jarvis himself seemed to wish to say something to Marianna, but his voice failed him, and he did not succeed in doing so; but Mrs. Jarvis was by no means so much oppressed, for she said in a loud voice, making quite certain that Aunt Shuter did not hear a word of it,— "I tell you what it is, Miss Marianna, you're living here by charity, you know that, or you ought to know it, and if you dare to say to this old mad woman that you ain't well used and perfectly happy, you shall go to the workhouse the first thing in the morning, and be made a slave of for life."

"Madam, I thank you," said the girl; "if it had not have been for the kindness of one person in this house, I should have preferred the mercy of that charity which the law would give me to that which is coldly doled out in this heartless house. I will not say I'm happy; why should I belie myself when I'm wretched?"

"Like the family," said the old woman, "like the family."

"Yes," exclaimed Job Brick, "I've heard as she's like the family; and I mean to say this, that if all the family are like her they're regular pancakes with sugar o' both sides and no mistake, for she's a trump—a one horse-shay on three wheels—a trivet with a hextra-leg—a brick!"

"Yes, yes, like the family. Now, my child, you must answer me what I write, or you can write whilst I speak—take the slate—are these people kind to you?"

"No," wrote Marianna upon the slate.

The old woman shook her head when she read the negative, and then said,—" I will take you away, but I will give £1,000 to any one here present who has said a kind word to you—write the name down upon the slate."

Marianna took the slate, and Selina advanced trippingly towards her. "Now, my dear, you know me, Selina, my dear, Selina you know, my dear, but you don't know one-half the kind things I intended to do for you."

" Oh, bother you!" said Hannibal; "I was going only this morning to order a little pony phaeton for her, with a turn-over seat behind for a footman in green plush, and two Hanoverian cream-coloured ponies."

" With the chill off, I suppose," said Job Brick.

" How dare you all speak!" cried Mrs. Jarvis. "My dear, you can tell your great aunt—for that's what she is, I suppose—that I've been a mother—quite a second mother—to you."

" Well, really, now, I think," said Mr. Jarvis, " as the expense of the establishment comes entirely out of my pocket, I ought to be considered a little in the business. Of course, Marianna, I can't say but you'll put down my name, but I've no objection in the world to say that I think you ought, when you come to consider all things."

" What's it all about," said Aunt Shuter, " what's it all about? the child can't move for you all. What do you mean by it? I'll cut you all off, as sure as fate, that I will!"

" 'I have no difficulty," said Marianna, as she took the slate, " in bestowing this one thousand pounds; I have no difficulty in choosing, for there is no competition in my mind upon this subject." As she spoke, she wrote in tolerably sized characters upon the slate the name of Job Brick, who, when he saw it, cried out,—

" Hip, hip, hip, hurrah! old Jarvis; I'll forgive you my fifteen bob for the next quarter's salary. I shall walk myself off now, and set up as a railway king. I don't see why I shouldn't as well as any other adventurer. Good bye to you all! I'll keep your secrets, for I don't want to crush you."

" Oh ah," said the old woman; " yes, yes, Job Brick. Are you Job Brick?" addressing Hannibal.

"Damn Job Brick!" said Hannibal.

"Well, I shan't stay here any more. I find she's like the family, so I shall take her away; and Job Brick, whoever he is, shall come too, and get his money—it's a very odd name, and will look funny on a cheque—'Pay Job Brick, Esq., one thousand pounds.' Yes, yes; come along, my dear—come along—I've got my carriage down stairs. People think I'm to be imposed upon, do they, because I'm a little hard of hearing? Yes, yes, we'll see about that."

"Confound you!" said Jarvis; "I don't know whether you can hear or not, but I only wish you may break your neck down the stairs, and then go to the devil."

"Yes, yes; I dare say you're saying something very civil, but it won't do, now, I tell you—not a bit of it—not a bit of it—so you may spare yourself."

"Really now," said Jarvis, "ought I to let this old woman take away the girl? No; I'll be hanged if I do! Old Bootle left her in my care, and in my care she shall remain; I'll baulk this old deaf devil somehow, for the girl shall not go."

"Hold!" said Mr. Gage, stepping into the room at that moment, "as I came up stairs I have heard something of what has passed— you have no power to detain the girl, Mr. Jarvis; this lady, if her name be Shuter, is a nearer relative; and as yet you will recollect you have no power under a will which has not been proved."

"And pray, sir, how came you here? Your presence is not wanted."

"My object in coming was to tell you that I value the proof of the legitimacy of Marianna Brotherton far beyond the twenty-five thousand pounds left to her in the will of old Mr. Bootle. I know that this eccentric old lady, Mrs. Shuter, will provide for her; and so I am willing to aid you in every possible way and shape in proving the marriage of Lucinda Bootle with Lieutenant Alexander Brotherton."

"Then it shall be proved. Let the old woman take this girl

H

with her, if she pleases—I care not—and recollect now, Mr. Gage, that there is now no subject of dispute between us."

" None whatever, sir; for once in a way you and I have a common object. I sincerely hope we may succeed in it, though, at the same time, I must tell you that if you had behaved to Marianna Brotherton with real care and kindness, you would have inherited a very large share, if not the whole, of Mrs. Shuter's property, which is about the same amount as Mr. Bootle's; but you have chosen your own course, Mr. Jarvis, and must abide by it."

As he spoke the attorney gave one hand to Mrs. Shuter and the other to Marianna, and so led them to the carriage.

Job Brick followed behind, but he did not like to leave the Jarvises quite so unceremoniously—he had been too long with them for that, so he paused upon the landing, and, holding the door open in his hand, addressed the assembled family,—

" You may all go to the deuce! and if you think I stayed along with you to do you any good, or because I liked you, you never were more mistaken in all your lives. I hate every one of you, and that's a fact. I shall write a book some of these days and put you all in it."

" Be off with you, be off!" cried Mr. Jarvis, "we don't want any of your insolence."

" Come, come," said Job, " none of that, or else—"

Job slipped up to Mr. Jarvis, and whispered a few words in his ear, which made him stagger, and turn a little faint.

" Ah!" said Job, " I thought I'd have you there; the fact is, I know something of every one of you—you all know I do, that's as clear as possible, so you daren't say a word. Take warning, all of you; we shall meet again next week."

Neither Mr. Hannibal nor the ladies seemed inclined to say anything to provoke the wrath of Job Brick, but they looked rather sheepish than otherwise; and when he gave a sort of circular nod, and turned on his heel to leave the room, it was a feeling of great relief that they saw him do so, and perhaps, upon the whole, when they came to consider the matter, they rather thought they were well rid of Job Brick, and probably that reflection reconciled them a little to his having the thousand pounds.

For a time, when the Jarvis family were left at home, there was a strange, awkward silence among them; for although they all felt that the little episode which had taken place was anything but an agreeable one, they knew not very well what to say to it.

Mr. Jarvis felt that events were thickening around him in an uncomfortable manner, and, without being able to positively affirm that there was anything amiss, he could not help feeling that nothing was exactly right—truly, his acquisition of fortune had done little towards his happiness.

" And pray, Mr. Jarvis," said his wife, " what was it that tha impertinent fellow said to you as he left the place ?"

" Nothing, nothing," said Mr. Jarvis, " nothing at all—at least, nothing of any consequence."

Mr. Jarvis hastily rose, and left the room : in a few moments more the banging of the street-door proclaimed that he had left likewise on another expedition, to try and get rid of mental consciousness by bodily fatigue.

———

CHAPTER XXI.

MR. BLOOMENBACK PROVES THE MARRIAGE.

IF anything could have tended more to induce Mr. Jarvis to wish the marriage proved between Lucinda Bootle and Lieutenant Brotherton, it certainly would have been the fact that old Mrs. Shuter had taken up so warmly the cause of Marianna.

He felt additionally angry on that ground against the orphan girl, and when he next saw Mr. Bloomenback he urged him in every possible way not to delay the proceedings which were necessary for the purpose of proving the legitimacy of Marianna. He began to think that it was a grand thing the lawyer had preserved the documents for that purpose, and the course of conduct that was adopted for the purpose of bringing those documents into existence was certainly of the most cunning and artful character.

The risk which had been incurred in extracting a leaf from the register of the little church of St. John, near Tetteridge, had been great, and had caused Mr. Jarvis many a shrinking, trembling sensation; but the idea of replacing the original leaf, and taking out the spurious one which had been introduced, seemed to him so fraught with danger as to be quite terrific.

And yet that was what Bloomenback proposed to do.

"You don't mean to say," remarked Jarvis, "that you really and truly will venture upon such a plan—is it not frightfully hazardous?"

"Everything of the sort is a little hazardous," said the lawyer, "but the bolder one sets about such things, certainly, the less is the hazard. You and I must go and do it: it's a £25,000 job between us, and you surely won't say that *that* is badly paid;—it must be done, and there is an end of it."

"But don't you recollect what hazard we were in before, and how we were forced nearly to kill a man before we could accomplish our purpose? You surely must recollect that, Bloomenback."

"I do; but I tell you, if we are obliged wholly to kill a man in undoing what we have done, we must not shrink from it; it is the only direct proof that can be obtained. You know very well, that when the affair was in agitation before, a large reward was offered to any parish clerk who would produce the registry of the marriage by old Mr. Bootle. We will offer another reward, and the registry shall be produced."

"And when do you purpose to do this?"

"To-night; let us get down at sunset. We will have none of your carriages or horses, for we must avoid the chances of future recognition. I know where to pitch upon a horse and gig on hire, which will take us down cleanly and comfortably."

"If it must be so, it must."

"There is no *must* in the case, you need not have it so unless you please. Pay the money, and make my half of it good to me, and you need do nothing of the sort."

"No, no, no, I cannot think of that; I will go with you, as you proposed. I know that in such transactions you have the devil's luck and your own."

"Management, management, Jarvis, it's all management: luck, indeed! it's the fashion for fools to accuse a clever fellow of luck, when he succeeds better than they do. Recollect, we meet at three at my chambers."

"Be it so, be it so; and what do you mean to do about the certificate of the marriage that you have?"

"Oh, as to that, I'll take care it shall be found somewhere; you will see that it shall turn up quite naturally, as collateral evidence, and, therefore, will materially aid the cause."

"Be it so, then, be it so. I must confess, Bloomenback, that it is by your aid and assistance I have got thus far on my road to fortune; and that, if we succeed in this, our last great enterprise, it will be all owing to your bold manœuvring."

"Well, well, one like's to have justice done one. Remember, at three, now. I have other business to attend to."

These two scheming men, who were so intent upon saving a sum which was really insignificant in comparison with that which they knew they could retain, met at the appointed hour at Bloomenback's chambers.

The lawyer was perfectly ready, and when he saw Jarvis, he became quite jocose, and said a great many pleasant things about punctuality being the soul of business, &c., and asked him if he had seen the one-horse chaise that was standing in Wych-street, with a bit of blood in it?

"The bit of what?" said Jarvis; "blood in a one-horse chaise!"

"Pho, pho! you know what I mean, the nag: I mean the nag, it'll whirl us down in no time; it's not far, you know, through Whetstone-gate."

"Oh, I understand, I understand. I know the spot well enough; we have been there before. I only wish it were over, and that the leaf of the registry was in its old accustomed place. Do you know that in all my drives and walks out of town, I have always most carefully avoided that spot: it seemed to me, if I did not, that something would soon happen to crush me and my fortunes."

"Ah! you're getting a little superstitious, but never mind that: come on, and let's be off, it will just be about dark by the time we get there, and then we must see what fortune will do for us in the way of opportunity."

They were soon in the chaise, and as the bit of blood certainly seemed impatient to be gone, they rattled along at a good pace, soon leaving the smoky city behind them, and emerging upon the Edgware-road, certainly one of the finest and best thoroughfares out of London.

Mr. Bloomenback was quite discoursive and gay; the rapid transit through the open air seemed to have a wonderfully beneficial effect upon his spirits, and he talked as if he were really a man free from the burdening effects of a cankered conscience, and yet what a world of iniquities had he not, from time to time, been guilty of —how many hearts had he professionally broken—how many widows had he rendered desolate, and how many orphans had he not robbed of their inheritance!

And yet this man could be merry and jocose, making sprightly remarks upon the little events of the journey, and indulging himself in many little stray bits of facetiæ with regard to what was going on on each side of the way. Did he expect to live for ever, that it was worth while to become a villain for twenty or thirty years, or more, in order that he might pass the rest of his life in jocund mirth and revelry?

How strange it is, that when men undertake complicated and rascally courses of action, they never recollect that life is too short to be tampered with, and by some strange hallucination of ideas never seem to discover that the history of all human nature has shown the discomfiture of such men, and that the time when they should begin to enjoy the ill-deserved fruits of their bad exertion never comes.

But no such train of reflections crossed the mind of either the lawyer or Mr. Jarvis, as they pursued their way towards Totteridge, for the purpose of undoing the piece of villany they had before done, and yet, strange to say, for an equally villanous purpose.

As Bloomenback had prophesied, they got down very quietly, and it wanted yet half-an-hour of sunset, or probably more, by the time they arrived at a little inn, not very distant from the church; there they put up the bit of blood and the chaise, and assuming, as much as possible, the airs and manners of persons who had merely come out for a little country air, by way of relaxation from business, they strolled gently, arm-in-arm, towards the church.

"Why do you tremble so?" said Bloomenback to Jarvis: "you manner alone is sufficient to show that you are upon some expedition of danger; come, come, be more of a man."

Jarvis made a ghastly effort to smile, and recover his composure, as the lawyer opened a little wicket-gate which led them into the churchyard, which was often resorted to by parties from London, on account of its extreme picturesque condition, and some curious antique tombs that were in it.

" Now," whispered Bloomenback, " just look about you, and seem to be studying the epitaphs; I really do not know what you can have to fear, and particularly now I desire you to be careful, for here's a fat fellow coming along the path-way, who looks like some official personage."

" Good evening, gentlemen," said a rather portly man, attired in a blue coat, drab-coloured shorts, worsted stockings, and high-lows; " good evening, gentlemen, a rummy-looking old church, built in the year 1000 and nothing, out of flint stones and mud, when William the Conqueror was a baby; burnt down, gentlemen, in 1403, in consequence of one of them ere old monks, as used to live in ecclesiastical places, setting light to his bed; beautified in 1823, and new railings put to the churchwarden's pew in 1826; the same day an old woman fell down and broke her leg, after saying that the weather-vane, at top of the steeple, was always wrong; named after John the 'Vangelist, who, I supposes, gentlemen, either built it, or was the first incumbrance, as they call it."

" Upon my word,' said Bloomenback, " you seem to be quite a walking chronicle of the old place."

" I is, gentlemen, and I ought to be—it's a very good thing, gentlemen; but sometimes, gentlemen, I am a walking about here of an evening, and meet gentlemen as has come down from London; they says to me quite natural, Can't we see the inside of it? says they, and then I gets the keys and shows 'em; and sometimes they gives me half-a-crown, and sometimes more, and now and then only a bob, and once in a way a tanner."

" But who are you, my friend, who have the power of showing the church in that way?"

" The beadle, to be sure—bless my heart! I thought every-body knew me; I'm the beadle of this ere place, and, in course, if anything is to be got by showing of it, who's most right to it, I should like to know? Why, gentlemen, I haven't been the beadle here above a year and a half, and you never see'd such a row in all your life as there was at the blessed election."

" Indeed !"

" Yes, gentlemen ; and I won it rather rum, for just as all was all going agin me, and I was a getting as queerly as possible, a friend of mine, he finds out that I weighed two stone and a half more than the other fellow; so we had bills printed with on the top of them, "wate" for thirteen stone, and let ten stone and a half wait till next time, and fat himself up like an Englishman afore he prespires to be a beadle, and that did the business, gentlemen, the other fellow hiding himself, and here I is."

"We, certainly," said Bloomenbeck, "have a great curiosity to see the inside of the church, and we don't mind a couple of half-crowns for the purpose of satisfying it."

"I'm as good as a conjuror," said the beadle, "I know'd it—this way, gentlemen, if you please, I've got the key in my pocket; I'll show you all the ins and outs of John the 'Vangelist, and, with ever sich a lot of reverence, you'll say it's a rummy-looking crib when you sees it."

They followed the beadle, who with a large key, that he took from a capacious pocket, opened a little, low, arch door, which led down by a step into the sacred edifice.

There was a chilly air, and a strange, silent aspect about the old place; the fading light of the day shone but faintly through some of the old stained windows, shadowing forth indistinctly some tombs, on which lay recumbent figures, roughly sculptured, but with all the marks of age upon them, and invested with that halo of antiquity, which is so pleasant to look upon.

Involuntarily they spoke low, and almost in whispers as they stood beneath the roof of that building, which for nearly a thousand years had been devoted to the service of Heaven; there must have been some singularity of association which could awe such a man as Bloomenback to silence.

"Listen to that," said the beadle, as he stamped his foot upon the flagstones that formed the paving, "listen to that, gentlemen, it's as hollow as a tea-chest, aint it? they say that underneath this very church is a place as big as the whole church itself."

"Vaults, I presume," said Jarvis, gathering courage to speak.

"Yes, sir, vaults, vaults, that's what it is, sir, and full of the dead; lots of old coffins, they say, there is down below and nothing but a few bones in them. Oh, gentlemen, doesn't it make one think of one's latter end, just to fancy now that people who walked about in their time, and gave half-crowns to beadles, is nothing but dust now."

" You're quite philosophical," said Bloomenback.

" Oh no, sir, I aint; I never interferes with the undertakering business; but, howsomever, gentlemen, here we is. That's the churchwarden's pew, and that ere one to the right belongs to old Mrs. Toddlegrub, a very respectable lady indeed; she never lets anybody that she don't know is living upon their own independent property sit down in her pew. This way, gentlemen, if you please —this way. Now, you'll get a fine view of the pulpit, and this little door leading into the westry."

" A very pleasant old place indeed," said Bloomenback. " Ah ! so this is the vestry, is it?—very nice, very nice. And what may this great box be ?"

" Oh, sir—that's, sir, what we call the parish chest; that's where the registry is kept, and all sorts of papers and books and things as has to be took care of."

" Oh, I understand, I understand—it's the parish strong box. Do you understand, Mr. J.? that's where the registry is kept—aint it funny ?"

Mr. Jarvis gave a ghastly grin, and said that he thought it was rather droll, while the corpulent beadle looked at them both, and seemed not to be very well able to make out what they were about, for he did not see anything funny in the parish chest.

———

CHAPTER XXII.

THE DECEIVED BEADLE.

"And so you've only been beadle for a year and a half?" said Mr. Bloomenback, breaking the somewhat awkward silence that had ensued.

"That's all, gentlemen, that's all; but I hopes to live long and do my duty. A year and a half aint much to try a man in; I hopes to get to fifteen stone yet afore I've done, and then, if any convulsion happens in the parish, I believe I shall be all right."

"Yes, you're a jolly looking sort of man, but don't you find that it's cold and chilling in this old church at times?"

"You're right there, sir, it is indeed; the old stones give out a coldness that's enough to chill one's blood. I'm often took with a sort of shiver in the middle of the service, and wish myself at home."

"Indeed! I'm taken with it now; but as I'm an old traveller to all parts of the country, I take care to carry with me a preservative against such effects. Look here, Mr. Beadle, what should you say this was?"

"Why, sir, I should say that looks remarkably like a flask bottle with something good in it to drink. Upon my life! sir, you know how to arrange things; it isn't everybody, now, that would have thought of that. Just out of curiosity now, sir, what may it be you've got there?"

"Why, my friend, it certainly ought to be some of the choicest brandy that ever any human being tasted. You see that the flask has a moveable cup at the bottom of it, which enables you to drink with ease, and as I feel that chilling sort of sensation coming on me, I don't see why I shouldn't indulge myself."

"Ah, yes," said the beadle, scratching his chin, "upon my life it's a very pleasant idea—very pleasant. I think, some of these days, I shall carry such a little flask myself."

By this time Mr. Bloomenback had poured out some of the

enticing liquid, and no doubt the beadle fully expected to see it poured down its owner's throat, but what an agreeable surprise it was to him when Mr. Bloomenback handed the cup to him, saying, " There's plenty of it—pray drink, Mr. Beadle ; there'll be enough for us all three."

" Well," said the beadle, as he quaffed off the contents of the little metal cup, " I must say that you is a gentleman every inch. You see, gentlemen, this is the westry, a comfortable room when there happens to be a fire lighted, and the mats all laid down on the floor ; and that 'ere is the parish chest, and this 'ere's the key of it, leastways it was the key; and so Mrs. King married the barber—thirteen stone.   And when we rings the bells, you should see how the old steeple shakes !   I don't know how you feel, gentlemen, but I aint exactly the thing; it isn't from what I've took either, but I'll sit down somehow—the idea of Spriggs calling that bear's grease : it's nothing but scented lard, and the last bear he killed was a pig.   Amen—please to remember the beadle—now you, sir, get off that 'ere grave-stone—respectable parishioners don't die for you to play at marbles on top of 'em—what a remarkable thing, the old church has changed into a great humming-top, and somebody's a spinning of it ?"

With these words the beadle's head sank upon his breast, and, as he had previously seated himself upon the floor, he after two or three ineffectual attempts to utter intelligible words, lapsed into dead silence, and his loud snoring soon proclaimed that he was fast asleep.

" So much for our friend the beadle !" said Bloomenback.

" Is he dead ?" whispered Jarvis.

" Dead ! nonsense."

" He has had a dose, however, which will last him for the next six-and-thirty hours ; but now for the work we have to do, and we may truly say with Macbeth, ' 'Twere well done, if 'twere done quickly.' "

" Then for Heaven's sake do it quickly," said Jarvis.   " I feel like a man standing upon a mine, who knows not a moment when the match may be placed to it and he may be blown to atoms."

"Indeed, you are more faint-hearted than even I thought you. I see that, as usual, I shall have to do all the work myself."

"Then why bring me here?"

"Because I was determined you should share the danger, if you did not share the labour."

While he spoke, Mr. Bloomenback had taken from the passive hands of the beadle the key which opened the parish chest, and in another moment the lid of that receptacle of parochial documents was thrown open, and the registry was at his mercy.

He knew the book again, for he had had it in his hands more than once, and, rapidly running over the leaves, he came to the one in question.

"Hold the book," he said to Jarvis, "hold the book, we shall have enough to do to perfect our job, before the twilight disappears."

With trembling hands Mr. Jarvis held the open book, while the attorney took from his pocket a small phial, containing a pale-coloured liquid ; by the assistance then of a camel's hair pencil, he spread a small streak of the liquid upon the edge of the leaf of the registry, which he wished to extract, close down to the binding. In another moment it came out, clean and easily, in his hands.

"Confound you!" he said to Jarvis, "you shake the book so with your trembling, I can hardly do the work."

Jarvis made no answer, but looked so ghastly pale, that he was evidently suffering the most intense anxiety. Then Bloomenback corked up the little phial carefully, and placed it in his pocket, from whence he took another, and then from the crown of his hat he produced the leaf of the registry which he wished to insert, in lieu of the one he had just extracted. Finally, then, touching its edge with a glutinous material that he had in the second bottle, he in a few moments perfectly succeeded in his object, and, taking the book from Jarvis, said,—

"It is done. Nothing but private information could induce any one to suppose that this volume had been tampered with. There will now be abundant proof of the marriage of Lucinda Doyle to Alexander Brotherton. The original leaf of the registry being restored, those who before have in vain searched this volume for that entry will, with amazement, now see it staring them in the face."

"Yes, yes," said Jarvis, anxiously, "come away—come away ! we surely need not stay another moment—now, for God's sake; come away: you—you can't think what an uncomfortable effect this place has upon me ; there must be something in the very air of a church that is a mute censure upon such deeds as these."

"Well," said Bloomenback, in a tone of wonder ; "on my life, Jarvis, if any one had told me such remarks as those would fall from your lips, I should have said they did not know you who made the statement: you astonish me beyond all precedent or possibility; why, what has come over you, man ; are you going to turn moral and sentimental ?"

"No, no, no ! come away—come away ; that is all I ask of you Bloomenback. Why tarry here, uselessly—what can you mean by it—do you court danger?"

"No, I'm ready to go; there, you see I've locked the parish chest, and placed the key again in the nerveless grasp of the stultified beadle—now, I'm ready; we've done our work, and done it famously."

Mr. Jarvis hurried along with the lawyer down the now darkened aisle of the church; he trembled at every step, and seemed as if he thought that the very echo of his tread would summon up some of the spirits of those who slept beneath to drive him to madness, with the stony glare of their death-like eyes.

"Come out of this—come out of this," he muttered. "I never liked a church at all, but least of all did I ever like it by night; and worse than night almost is this, for there is just light enough left to see strange shadows, and to fancy almost anything."

"Well," said Bloomenback, "thank the Fates, I never gave my mind to superstition."

They reached the church-door, and emerged into the open air. Oh, what a great relief it was to Jarvis to do so : his frame seemed to expand, and he moved onward like a man from whose breast a heavy weight has been lifted.

" I'm glad it's done—I'm glad it's done," he said ; " and, after all, what we've done to-day, you know, Bloomenback, is rather right than wrong, because the girl is legitimate, and we are proving that she is so."

" But what do I care, whether it is right or wrong, so that it answers our purposes ? but, hush ! here's somebody coming."

A woman came hurriedly along the path, and when she met them, she said,—

" Pray, gentlemen, have you seen anything of Mr. Swigs ?"

" We have not the happiness of his acquaintance," said Bloomenback; " pray, who is Mr. Swigs ?"

" My husband, the beadle."

" We much regret we can give you no information ; but, perhaps, he has slipped into some snug old family vault—it's a matter of taste, you know, he may have done so : was he a remarkably thin, little, old man, with a sharp countenance ?"

There was something in the lawyer's manner which induced the woman to see that he was jesting with her ; and she walked on, muttering something not of a very complimentary character, as regarded the lawyer and Mr. Jarvis.

" For Heaven's sake," said Jarvis, " get away—get away, quickly ; or that woman will be after us."

" Oh, nonsense. I slammed the door of the church, and Swigs is a prisoner ; there is no danger, for he will sleep too soundly to call for aid ; this is a nice, salubrious, airy place,— what say you to hiring a couple of beds at the inn, and staying till morning? I think it wouldn't be a bad move—just to compose your nerves, you know."

" Oh no; no," said Jarvis, " this jesting is very ill-timed : let us to town at once I shall know no peace until some miles are placed between me and this old church."

Bloomenback laughed in his usual quiet way, for he certainly had not the least intention of remaining ; they walked rapidly to the inn, at the door of which stood the horse and chaise ; and stopping the bit of blood in a very luxurious meal of wet hay, which he was indulging in, they, in three minutes more, were proceeding at the rate of a good ten miles an hour towards London.

Then, indeed, Mr. Jarvis breathed a little freely, and when he saw the gas-lights and heard the hum of the great city, he spoke in something like his usual manner, as he said,—"Yes, yes, we have saved £25,000, at all events we have saved that, Bloomenback, and I begin to feel quite easy and comfortable again—it was rather a nervous thing, wasn't it?"

"Yes, if you choose to make it so," said Mr. Bloomenback; by the chancellor's wig, I don't know what you'd do without me!"

CHAPTER XXIII.

THE MEETING AT THE PRIORY.

IT is morning again, and Mr. Jarvis awakens to what may be most emphatically called "another day of troubles." When he returned from St. John's Church with Mr. Bloomenback, he had proceeded direct to his own home, and then, partly because he was well pleased at the termination without an accident of the adventure he had gone through, and partly because he felt nervous and excited, he sat down to do the very last thing he should have thought of doing, viz., to drink wine; and the consequence was, that he got up in the morning with a superadded-disagreeable-no-trifling-one-to-think-of-an-alarming head-ache. He had all that wretched feeling of mental prostration when he arose, which, by ordinary folks, is summed up in the saying, that such and such a person feels perfectly ready and willing to give his life for a farthing.

And truly everything to Mr. Jarvis seemed to be stale, flat, and unprofitable: a man more wretched than he was, with what he considered the certainty at all events of £7,500 a year, could not have been found under any circumstances whatever.

He almost regretted, as happy times gone past, that period when he first commenced business in Bishopsgate, and was struggling against deficient capital, and all the troublesome and untoward events which such a circumstance gives rise to.

What were his anxieties then, in comparison to what they are now? It is true that now and then he was robbed of a few hours' repose by uneasy considerations about some acceptance coming due with the alarming rapidity that acceptances are wont to exhibit, but what was that in comparison now to the almost unceasing worry of mind that he endured? He could not help looking at himself in his dressing-glass, and mentally owning that he looked a ten-years-older man since the news had first struck upon his ears that old Bootle was no more; and yet that was an event that he had been so striving for—a something that he had been looking forward to, as the heir-apparent to a crown waits anxiously for the trumpet-blast which proclaims him the successor of the monarch who has just subsided into the sleep of death.

But we need not enlarge upon the many miseries of such a man as Jarvis: his sufferings lie upon the surface, and are very easily seen and scanned; moreover, he finds that he has little to do but to wait with a passive sort of endurance the progress of events; for, as Mr. Bloomenback had nothing else of a dangerous character to perform, he was not at all anxious or insisting upon Jarvis taking part in it.

The lawyer came to him in the morning, and after rallying him upon his bad looks, which, Heaven knows, were sufficiently apparent, he took a newspaper from his pocket, and showed him an advertisement offering a reward of £20 to any one who could offer irrefragable and undeniable evidence of the marriage of Lucinda Bootle to Alexander Brotherton, a lieutenant in the army, who were supposed to have been united, so the advertisement said, at some little church in the immediate vicinity of London.

" Don't you think now, friend Jarvis," said Bloomenback, "that this will set all the parish clerks within twenty miles of the metropolis on the hunt? Don't you fancy that we shall pretty soon have a communication dated from St. John's Church, near Totteridge, to the effect that it is in that quarter the twenty pounds must go?"

" Yes, and our friend, the beadle, will most probably recognise us."

" Well, if he does, the consequences of his getting drunk in the church (for that is what it will look like) will fall on his head, not ours. But our friend the beadle, as you call him, will have nothing to do with it; it is the parish clerk, who will receive as his reward the twenty pounds, and with whom we shall have to deal. Beadles are not allowed exactly to slip into such good things, so do not suppose it; a certificate will be brought to us signed by the present curate or vicar of the parish, and that is all we shall require. If Mr. Gage does not think that evidence sufficient, he can go down and examine the register himself."

" Then you think it is all safe ?"

" I not only think, but I am certain it's all safe; there can be no manner of doubt upon the subject : within three days' time I would chance my life to a ten-pound note that the reward will be claimed."

" Well, Bloomenback, I must confess you manage these matters adroitly."

" Nonsense, I don't want any compliments—it's cash that I work for; and now, the moment we do get an answer to the advertisement, it will be our duty to make Mr. Gage acquainted with the fact, in order that he may pursue what line of conduct he pleases consequent thereupon."

The lawyer was perfectly correct; for, on the evening of the second day, he came again to Jarvis, and triumphantly laid before him a copy of the registry, which had been furnished by the parish clerk of the place, and duly attested by the signature of the curate.

" There," he said, " there, Jarvis—the twenty-five thousand pounds are saved, and Mr. Gage, who was so very solicitous that this thing should be proved, will surely now be satisfied. It is to be sincerely hoped that he will not alter his opinion, and begin to fancy that a spurious reputation, as regards birth, is extremely well paid for at so high a rate. Are you not well satisfied, Jarvis, now ?"

" Of course I am, or at least I know I ought to be. I owe

much to you, Bloomenback, and I almost begin not to grudge the enormous reward you have named for yourself."

" Well," said Bloomenback, with a satisfied air, " that is as it should be ; of course it don't make much difference, only one certainly does prefer people being satisfied to their grumbling. I've taken the slight liberty, Jarvis, of sending a note to Mr. Gage to meet me here, in order to place this little interesting memorandum, which staves off the twenty-five thousand pounds' legacy in his hands."

" Then is he coming here ?"

" Yes ; and that knock at the door, I should say, proclaims his presence. What are you afraid of ? In all my life, Jarvis, I never knew a man so full of fears as you ; you seem to have lost all capacity to meet people, or to face the slightest uncomfortable circumstance, and I am the more surprised at that, because you certainly were not wont to be so squeamish."

" It is of no use blaming me, I am nervous ; while there is anything to do I can do it, but it is success that has unnerved me. I never, as you must know, expected all old Bootle's money."

" Well, but having got it all, you should be the better pleased ; but hush ! here comes one of your footmen, and we shall soon know if this be really our friend Gage or not."

There was no Job Brick now to announce the visitors, and consequently one of the footmen did the duty as page of the reception-room. Mr. Gage's card was brought upon a silver salver to the drysalter, who desired, in rather a faint voice, that the gentleman might be shown up.

" Now mind what you're about," said Bloomenback to Jarvis, " and don't put on that abominable look, as if you had just stolen something and were trying to escape the officers of justice."

" I will be careful—I will be careful."

Mr. Gage in another moment made his appearance, and certainly there was nothing so very alarming about his general aspect, that ought to have induced Mr. Jarvis to put himself out of the way ; but how true it is, that a guilty conscience needs no accuser : it was not Mr. Gage that was Rhododendron Jarvis's enemy ; it wa not Marianna Brotherton that he dreaded, or any one of the people whom through a long life of iniquity he had wronged; but it was his own heart that stood up as his accuser—it was his own conscience that made him a coward, and which forced him to feel that he had no right to hold up his head among men of honesty and worth.

Mr. Gage, however, was welcomed by Bloomenback with an amount of coolness and self-possession that was the envy, if it was not the admiration, of Rhododendron Jarvis.

"Sir," he said, "I dare say you were surprised at hearing from me in such very urgent and pressing terms, but you will please to remember that we are now transacting business of really vital importance, and, unless I very much mistake, you will not be very sorry to hear that we are now actually in possession of proofs of the legitimacy of the young girl, Marianna Brotherton, in whose welfare you have taken so kindly an interest."

"I am not sorry to hear you say so," replied Mr. Gage, "and I here repeat my former declaration, viz., that I look upon the proof of the marriage of Lucinda Brotherton as a far more gratifying and important circumstance than the legacy in old Mr. Bootle's will;—pray what is your proof, gentlemen?"

"The church registry, and there it is."

Mr. Gage read it with critical attention, and Bloomenback, who looked at him curiously while he did so, saw that he was struggling to conceal a great amount of emotion.

"You seem affected, sir," he said.

"I am rather surprised than affected," said Mr. Gage. "Lucinda Brotherton always insisted that she was married at the church from whence this certificate is dated, and yet, although I myself, as well as others, looked carefully over the registry, strange to say we found no such entry."

"Ah!" said Bloomenback, carelessly, "these things will happen: I recollect myself an instance of a couple of leaves being stuck together accidentally in a church registry in the country; and the consequence was, that estates worth nearly half a million of money changed hands for a couple of years until the accident was discovered."

"Well, well," said Mr. Gage, "it may be so; I'm not one who is disposed to poison a pleasant pleasure, because it did not come before; perhaps, gentlemen, you are not indisposed to allow me to take with me this document, and I have the pleasure to inform you, that Mr. Smith, who has the will of the deceased Mr. Bootle, will be in town on Monday week, and I propose that on that day we meet at the Priory, the late Mr. Bootle's residence in Wilts; for it is under that roof, it appears to me, the will ought to be read, and nowhere else."

"Very good," said Mr. Bloomenback; "in that case, then, Mr. Jarvis can put his seals upon the property, and I ask you now, Mr. Gage, if you do not admit that, in consequence of the legitimacy of Marianne being proved, she loses her legacy?"

"In law, I am compelled to admit she does; and I very much doubt if, under the circumstances, she would get any relief in equity. I do not, in my own mind, think she would; but all that does not so much matter, because it seems that old Mrs. Shuter has taken a fancy to provide for the girl, and, in that case, she certainly can want for nothing."

"Mr. Gage," said Bloomenback, "you're a sensible man, sir; and it is an extremely gratifying thing to me and my client to have to do business with a professional gentleman who takes such correct views of the subjects brought under his notice. On Monday week we shall do ourselves the pleasure, most certainly, of being at the Priory. It will be a melancholy thing for my friend Jarvis; but, as you say, I think it looks but respectful to the deceased, and it is but proper to all parties that the will should be read beneath the roof of the late Mr. Bootle's house."

"Then, gentlemen," said Mr. Gage, rising, "it will be in Wiltshire, and I shall have the extreme satisfaction, at all events, of telling Mrs. Shuter that her niece is not the base-born girl she has been insinuated to be; and I hope, Mr. Bloomenback, you will not forget that I was to have a thousand pounds."

"Oh, not at all—not at all. Jarvis, I think you ought to give Mr. Gage your cheque at once for the amount."

Jarvis hesitated, and then Mr. Gage intimated that he was

quite willing to take Mr. Jarvis's acknowledgment for the amount, if it were more convenient for that gentleman to give it, than the cash immediately; and to this arrangement Mr. Jarvis at once acceded; so that Mr. Gage fairly walked off with an I O U for one thousand pounds in consideration of services which, we suspect, both Mr. Bloomenback and Mr. Jarvis will ultimately consider were of an exceedingly equivocal character as regarded them.

There was a look of great satisfaction upon the face of Mr. Gage as he reached the street.

"So at length," he said, "these scoundrels have fairly outwitted themselves. At every turn their avarice has defeated them. Had they possessed one spark of kindly feeling in the whole transaction, they would have been saved; but, as it has happened from first to last, there has been nothing but cold, calculating avarice, and the tissue of crimes which they have become involved in, they will now find it impossible to extricate themselves from. Truly, Mr. Rhododenderon Jarvis, you stand upon the edge of a most frightful precipice, and over you must go, if others have not far more mercy upon you than you have ever had upon anybody in all your life!"

Mr. Bloomenback was rather of a different opinion, for, when he was alone with Jarvis, he gave him a great blow upon the back, that was rather more hearty than pleasant, as he said,—

"Triumph! triumph, Jarvis! Have we not done it now? Who shall now say nay to your ambitious hopes and projects? You may consider yourself, Rhododendron, as at the commencement of a new existence—an existence teeming with life, beauty, and sunshine. You can have your carriages, your horses, your servants, and your hounds of every degree, including the most slavish of all — the sycophant, who will crawl into your presence to tell you, with a silvery adulation in every tone, that you're everything you are not."

"And you too," said Jarvis, as he rubbed his two cold hands together, and shivered slightly—"and you too, Bloomenback, you can do the same, you know!"

"Yes, perhaps I can; and perhaps I do not choose. I like

power,—I like to be able to let people see what I can do if I please. If all the world had but one neck I should like to put my heel upon it, and I shall do it, for the world will allow of such things, provided the heel be tipped with gold."

"You're a strange fellow!"

"I know I am—but let that pass. There's about eight days yet to enjoy yourself in, before we shall meet at the Priory in Wilts. Don't let them hang so heavy on you as on the last eight, for, by Heaven! if you do so, there'll be nothing of you left."

CHAPTER XXIV.

THE OLD MANSION.

THE eight days had passed away, and, to all appearance, Mr. Jarvis had to the letter followed the advice of Bloomenback with a desperate sort of recklessness. He seemed to have thrown off all care; and whereas before he had been shrinking and timid in the use of the almost boundless wealth he felt himself heir to, he now, with a wild and lavish extravagance, bustled his way in the great world, as if he indeed felt that he had little time to lose.

In defiance of all ordinary decency—for he ought to have assumed a little grief at the death of the man who had behaved so munificently to him, even if he had felt it not—he made his magnificent house a scene of riot and confusion, from sunset almost till the break of day.

He was making great efforts to try to persuade himself that he was enjoying his money. Alas, poor Jarvis! the greater the effort the greater the failure; the canker-worm of care at his heart would not be stilled in its writhings because he gave an entertainment every evening. He still knew that he was grasping the wealth which he had obtained by the grossest deceit—he still knew that it was by the traduction of the innocent he had attained his present position—he could not conceal from himself that if there was a retribution in this world, or a judgment in the next, he of all was most amenable to both.

He certainly had succeeded in carrying to his lips the golden draught he had so much longed for; but, as the price of so doing, he had been compelled to allow to be mixed with it some drops of poisonous essence, which deprived it of its colour and beauty.

Unhappy Jarvis! he actually envied a great lump of a footman he had, in whose large, staring, vacant countenance not a line of care had ever made its appearance, or was ever likely to do so; and, what was more extraordinary, probably Thomas in the yellow plush did not envy his master.

But the eight days did at length pass away, and Mr. Jarvis tried to get up a pleasant feeling in his mind by making grand preparations for his journey to Wilts. He made the offer to Mrs. Jarvis to accompany him, which she at once accepted; but Hannibal and Selina, to whom likewise a similar offer was made, politely declined it, intimating to their paternal relative that they were by far too much occupied in the *beau monde* of London to think of just then leaving the metropolis.

Truly, to use one of Mrs. Jarvis's elegant expressions, it might be said that the young people had other fish to fry. It was not likely that the Honourable Colonel Mildmay and the equally Honourable Georgiana Damer, having hooked their prey, would allow it so easily to escape; and so we may expect to hear of some very important results ensuing from the clever and very admirable manner in which they angled their victims. Had we not other and more important concerns in hand, connected with the incidents of our story, we might feel inclined to follow the fortunes of this precious quartette; but as it is, we shall satisfy ourselves with the production of certain results that ensue from this great insight that Hannibal and his sister Selina were getting into fashionable society.

By nine o'clock on the morning of that Monday when the meeting was to take place at the Priory, the early loiterers in Park Lane might have observed a very stylish barouche, with four most magnificent grey horses, at the door of one of the most *recherché* houses in that vicinity.

And this equipage, with all its gorgeous addenda, was kept waiting long enough for everybody to see it, and for many a question to be put with regard to whose it was, and many an answer returned, to the effect that it belonged to the great Mr. Jarvis. We do not, in his present state of mind, exactly accuse Rhododendron Jarvis of this petty piece of vanity, for he was certainly ready to depart precisely at nine o'clock; but Mrs. Jarvis thought that it would be just as well, as they had gone to the expense of four horses and a couple of postilions, that the neighbours should, at all events, be allowed about twenty minutes' time in which to vex themselves with the show.

The distance to the Priory at Wilts, even going at the slashing pace which Mr. Jarvis's means could command, was such that six hours must elapse before the wheels of the travelling carriage could press the green sward in front of that noble mansion. Mr. Bloomenback had arrived in good time, for—although by force of coming in for half of Jarvis's good fortune, he might count himself as good a man—it was no small congratulation to him to undertake the journey at Rhododendron's expense.

There was quite a benign smile upon the face of Bloomenback when they started, and even Jarvis could not help feeling a sort of exhilaration at that rapid transit through the air which the dashing grey horses promised for him.

And, let people say what they will of quiet, half-sleepy, pedestrian tours, or of jogging through a long journey on a serious pony, there is something which stirs the blood, and makes the fancy vigorous, in that rapidity of movement which is procured without fatigue; and as it is a well-known fact that any continuous sound of one character has a tendency to soothe the nervous system, so even the rumble of the wheels, and the slight noise which the vehicle made upon its well-hung springs, served to restore Jarvis to a state of equanimity.

I

The balmy fresh air of morning blew coldly in his face, but there was life and vigour in every breath of it, so that, after a time, he could turn to Bloomenback and make some pleasant remark, which was replied to by one of the quiet, half-subdued laughs of the lawyer, while Mrs. Jarvis had assumed what she considered an uncommonly aristocratic attitude, which displayed, to the best advantage, a richly embroidered mantle that she wore, on which she took care to lay one of her fat and red hands, in order that the glittering gems which adorned her fingers might not escape observation.

We have little to do with the incidents of the road. The day was all that could be wished, and, before they had gone twenty miles, Jarvis seemed almost a new man, so much had he recovered from the nervousness that had beset him previous to their departure.

But this salubrious and pleasant state of things was not to last. He had been nervous and apprehensive of he knew not what, before he started; the fresh air and the excitement of the journey for a time conquered those feelings; but, as the great city was left far behind, and when, about three o'clock or half-past, they saw some stately towers and tall trees, which announced the immediate vicinity of the Priory, all the coward feelings of Jarvis came back to him, and he trembled like a leaf shaken by the autumn wind.

There was a look of slight anxiety, too, upon the countenance of Bloomenback, and Mrs. Jarvis was silent, from curiosity and wonder, as the carriage dashed up a broad avenue of stately lime trees, and they caught occasionally glimpses of the superb old mansion, which formed part of the property of the late Mr. Bootle.

There was a strange air of silence and desolation about the place, so that Jarvis could not help thinking that, upon the death of its proprietor, the servants must have found it lonesome and fled from it; at all events, he felt that he could never live in those stately halls.

Scarcely had the carriage drawn up at the principal entrance, whc the hall door was opened, and Mr. Gage made his appearance, with all the aspect as if he had been watching the arrival of the party most interested in the events of the day.

He cared but little, and that little was not of a very welcome or commendatory character; but he let the Jarvises know, that if they followed him he would take them to some place called the Painted Parlour, where Mr. Smith, with the will, was waiting their coming.

And now, it was rather amusing to see Mrs. Jarvis, who resented the cavalier-like manner in which they were received, and who was determined to let the one footman know, by implication, who and what she was.

"Ah!" she said, "I shall have all this place altered. I've no idea of filling up the hall with stags' horns, and skins of wild beasts, and guns; and I hate stony pavements; do you hear, young man? I'm going to have this place boarded."

The footman looked a long way over Mrs. Jarvis's head, and made no reply; upon which she immediately gave him a month's notice, commencing from that day, and told him he should pretty soon find out who was mistress there, and who was master.

Mr. Bloomenback evidently quite enjoyed this little episode; but Jarvis paid no attention to it, for as Mr. Gage walked on, he felt himself, as it were, compelled to follow him, and so they at last reached a stately room of the olden time, on the ample hearth of which some burning logs were smouldering, mingled with huge lumps of bright sea-coal, that blistered and hissed, and sent forth their jets of flame, right merrily. In an old arm-chair, by the fire-side, sat Mrs. Shuter, and standing close to her was a remarkably thin, small man in black.

Mr. Jarvis rather recoiled, and so did Mr. Bloomenback; for they certainly neither of them had expected exactly to see the lady at the Priory, although there was nothing improper in her being there, or unlikely, considering the business that that day had to be transacted.

She paid not the slightest attention to the new-comers; but the small gentleman in black bowed, and Mr. Gage whispered to Jarvis, "That is Mr. Smith."

Jarvis bowed likewise, and so did Bloomenback; and then, after some little bustle, the party was seated, and Mr. Smith, stepping forward, said, in a clear, soft voice,—

" Being in possession of the last will and testament of Mr. Bootle, I have peculiar pleasure in meeting the parties interested, who are now, I perceive, with one exception, all here,—oh, that exception is made up."

These latter words arose from the fact of the door being suddenly opened, and Marianna Brotherton gliding in.

" I shall proceed," continued Mr. Smith, drawing a folded paper from his pocket, " to read the short and concise will of my deceased friend; and as there cannot be too many witnesses to the reading of such a document, may I request that such servants as happen to be in the house should be permitted to be present?"

" Certainly," said Mr. Gage, " I will order that."

" Stop, sir, if you please," said Mrs. Jarvis; " I orders every thing here. I believe I know what's what, and a trifle beyond it. I don't know who brought this little brat of a Marianna to the house, but whoever did so had better take her back again as soon as possible, for I won't have her here—get out of the way, will you? I'll ring myself. John, send the servants here."

When the servants did collect, they did not seem many in number; there was the old housekeeper and a younger looking female who kept behind her, and there was John, the supercilious footman, and behind him several male figures. Mrs. Shuter, at this juncture, gave Mr. Bloomenback rather a severe blow on the head with her slate, as an intimation to him to give her his serious attention, and then she handed him the slate, on which he might write, saying,—

" What are they all about? You lawyers are such thieves that one likes to know what you're doing."

"Much obliged," said Bloomenback; and he wrote upon the slate in large letters,—

"They're going to dissect a dead donkey."

"Oh, thank you," said Mrs. Shuter, when she had read it; "*you* seem to be alive yet, as far as I can see."

Mr. Bloomenback found he had rather met his match, so he said no more, and Mr. Smith commenced reading the will :—

"I declare this to be the last will and testament of myself, Jeremiah Bootle, of the Priory, in the County of Wilts, and it pleases me to bequeath the whole of my estate, real and personal, to Mr. Rhododendron Jarvis, of Bishopsgate Within, in the City of London, Drysalter, to have and to hold for his sole benefit and use, without any deduction whatsoever, except the payment of such just debts as may be proved against my estate to the satisfaction of the said Rhododendron Jarvis, and my funeral expenses, which I desire may be made as small as possible, so as to be at all consistent with my position in the county."

"A very sensible old man," said Mrs. Jarvis; "I was afraid all along he'd be putting us to no end of expense about his funeral."

"Codicil, No. 1."

Jarvis gave a deep groan as he faltered out,—

"Is there a codicil No. 2?"

"There is certainly," said Mr. Smith, "although I cannot say that I consider it of much importance; but you shall hear codicil No. 1 :—'I bequeath to Marianna Bootle, the child of my deceased daughter Lucinda, the sum of twenty-five thousand pounds, to be paid out of my estate within one month from my decease?'

"Codicil, No. 2.—'Whereas, I have read a learned paper on death by a profound German philosopher, Doctor Slausberghausen, in which he proves that many persons are buried when they are actually only in a state of collapse: I require that my body be kept for thirty days after my presumed decease, and that, if I then show no signs of animation, I be buried.'

"What!" exclaimed Jarvis; "do you mean to tell me he is not buried yet?"

"No," said Mr. Smith, solemnly, "he's only in the next room."

"The devil!"

Mrs. Shuter gave Bloomenback another severe blow with the slate, and he cried.—

"Good God! somebody that knows this old woman, come and explain to her what's going on, or else she'll be the death of me."

"I'm your sort," said Job Brick, suddenly making his appearance from the crowd at the door-way; "I'll do it; she's made me her major domus;" and Job, as he spoke, took the slate and wrote upon it, that "the dead body of Mr. Bootle was in the next room," which seemed to satisfy her.

"Well, gentlemen," said Bloomenback, "I presume our business is over, and I've only to say in behalf of my client, Mr. Jarvis, that he will be quite ready to pay the twenty-five thousand pounds whenever such a person as Marianna Bootle makes her appearance."

"I quite understand," said Mr. Smith, "to what you allude—the legitimacy of the young lady being proved; which my friend, Mr. Gage, tells me, raises the point with regard to her description in the will. I cannot say that, under the circumstances, I think that description is sufficient; and I doubt if any professional man will undertake the case; but I appeal to you, Mr. Jarvis, as the inheritor of a princely fortune, to say what you will give to Marianna. Of course you feel and know, that in any case Mr. Bootle meant fully and simply to provide for her—will you give her the £25,000, and so do an act of justice along with one of generosity?"

"Certainly not," said Jarvis; "let Mrs. Shuter take care of her."

"Sir, I can tell you that Mrs. Shuter is penniless; she is a harmless lunatic, and has but a small annuity secured to her by the late Mr. Bootle, long ago. But in her madness she fancies herself rich, and she keeps up that strange mental delusion by carrying about with her bank notes of a very high denomination, as she supposes them to be, but they are in reality hair-dressers' puffs belonging to the Bank of Elegance—so that Marianna Brotherton is indeed destitute."

"It don't matter to us," said Mrs. Jarvis, "money's money. She can go to service, or do what she likes; we've got children of our own to provide for."

"Yes," said Jarvis, as he wiped his face, for the perspiration stood upon it; "yes, we've got children of our own to provide for and we'll give nothing."

"That is very sad," said Mr. Smith, "for nothing can be endered."

"I—I—I think," said Mrs. Shuter, as she rose, "I think I'll go and see poor dear old Bootle before they put him under ground. What do I want with his money?—I don't want his money: I've got money enough of my own—thousands upon thousands."

"Ah!" said Job, "she's a poor old brick, and as much as possible: I'll go with her."

"Once more," said Mr. Smith, "let me appeal to you, Mr. Jarvis, in behalf of this destitute girl."

"I will do nothing, sir," said Jarvis, stung almost to madness as he was by the reiterated request; "I will do nothing. Damnation, sir! don't I tell you I'll do nothing?"

"Hark!" said Mr. Gage, "what new arrivals have we now? I hear the sound of carriage wheels, and what a peal that is at the hall door!"

There was, indeed, a thundering demand for admission to the Priory, and a general feeling of curiosity seemed to invest every one to know who the arrivals could consist of.

In a few moments there was heard the tramp of several feet—the door of the apartment was flung open, and Selina Jarvis made a theatrical rush into the room, and flung herself at her mother's feet, exclaiming,—

"I'm married—I'm married! I'm Lady Mildmay now—honoured parents forgive, and—and——"

"Come down with something handsome," said Colonel Mildmay

popping his head in at the doorway. "Ah, Jarvis! how d'ye do? Mrs. J.—your most obedient—quite a family party, I declare! Upon my word, these are pleasant, delightful little meetings! Come now, governor-in-law, what are you going to stand?"

"Stop!" cried Hannibal Jarvis, making his appearance, "before that question's decided, allow me to say a word,—I'm married too; the Honourable Georgiana Damer is my lovely bride—she is here!"

"Yes, oh yes!" exclaimed the lady alluded to, as she made a dramatic bound into the apartment, and clung round the neck of Rhododendron Jarvis before he could help himself. "Ah, my dear sir, the cloud-capped towers, the gorgeous palaces!—twenty thousand down is all we ask to make us happy."

"Twenty thousand devils!" said Jarvis; "what is the meaning of all this?"

"Why, it seems to me," said Mr. Gage, "that your children have got married without asking your leave."

"Married!" said Mrs. Jarvis, "I'm ready to sink."

"But my wife's a lady in her own right," said Hannibal, "an honourable."

"And my husband's a *kernel*," cried Selina.

"A what?"

"Well, ladies and gentlemen," said Mr. Smith, "I don't know about honourables or dishonourables, but I certainly was engaged in London a good while ago in a theatrical case, arising out of an assault, and then this young lady appeared as Miss Muggins, of the Eagle, in the City-road."

Hannibal sat down on the floor, and deliberately pulled out a handful of his hair; Mrs. Jarvis shrieked; and Rhododendron staggered to a chair, where he sat, looking like the ghost of Banquo at Macbeth's feast.

"And if I am Miss Muggins," said the Honourable Miss Georgiana Damer, "you little sneaking, poor, low-brought-up, half-famished-looking vagabond, what's that to you?"

"I regret," said Mr. Smith, "to be the agent of making disagreeable discoveries; but if I do not much mistake, the gentleman who calls himself Colonel Mildmay is named Harry Brotherton, whom the police have been looking for during the last half-dozen years on various charges of theft and forgery."

Selina sat down by the side of her brother, and beat upon the floor with her heels, like drumsticks. She quite forgot that one half of the curls on each side of her face were false, and the moment she touched them, away they all came together.

"Curse you all!" said Rhododenderon Jarvis, springing to his feet; "as you have made your beds, you shall lie upon them. I discard you from this moment forthwith. I will not have another word to say to any of you; but with my immense fortune—I say with my immense fortune——"

"Stop a bit," said Job Brick, as he glided into the room, and gave Rhododenderon Jarvis a nudge with his elbow—"stop a bit. old file; don't be hard on little Marianna; give her something, now; and your own children, too, give them a trifle. Say a kind word of somebody or something."

"Not a sixpence!" cried Jarvis, foaming with rage; "everybody may be damned."

"Hush! hush!" said Job Brick; "don't use such words, my own hair's standing upon end as it is, in consequence of something else. You won't believe it, any of you, when I tell you; but when poor old Aunt Slater and I got into the next room, and she saw the dead body of old Mr. Bootle, I thought the old woman's heart would have broken. There he was, laid out in his snuff-coloured coat and top-boots, just as he used to wear when he was alive. Come, now, Jarvis, give something to Marianna, if it's only one thousand pounds, give it her."

"Not a rap—not a rap."

"Well, well, I saw the old lady's tears fall upon the dead man's face, and—that recovered him!"

Jarvis staggered back, and dashed his hand through a window in his efforts to get something to hold by. A pair of folding doors were flung open, and Mr. Jeremiah Beetle, pale and anxious, and with the traces of deep emotion on his countenance, tottered into the room.

"The drama is over," he said; "Rhododendron Jarvis, I have found out who and what you are—cold, selfish, and criminal! My child—my Marianna—come to my arms! My child's child—my darling—my beautiful!"

He sank upon a seat, and Marianna, sobbing, wound her arms around him. There was an awful stillness in the place then; for some there present were paralysed with wonder, while others were in a like state from terror; and some were still, because they felt the sacredness of the old man's feelings.

As for the Jarvises, no pen could depict the absolute agony that sat upon their countenances; and when Mr. Gage now stepped forward with a bright flush upon his face and spoke, Rhododendron seemed to shrink, as it were, within himself and to cower before him.

"It is my pleasant and agreeable task," said the attorney, "to unravel some of the mysteries in which this transaction has been involved. I have always doubted even the apparent evidence of my own senses against the marriage of Lucinda; but the subject became an interested one with Mr. Beetle, and I felt that if there was any mystery in the matter, it was Mr. Jarvis and his accomplice, Bloomenback, who alone could unravel it. I had a friend in Job Brick, who has worked manfully with me for the right. Job Brick is the son of an old friend of mine, and consented to act the part he has done for the cause of truth and justice. His real name is Algernon, and he has received a classical education."

Rhododendron Jarvis panted as if he wanted more air, and the attorney continued,—

"The marriage of Lucinda with Lieutenant Brotherton, which was my grand object, has been proved. I shall not advise Mr.

Bootle to inquire further into that transaction; and the fact that the sel-ishness of the Jarvises is likewise proved, I fully expected, but was not so anxious about. If Mr. Jarvis had given anything to Marianna (and he had abundant chances given him), the same amount would have been handed to Paul by Mr. Bootle, but now he gets nothing, and I shall sue both Jim and Bloomenback to give thousand pounds, for which I hold their bills. Truth has triumphed."

"Lor, you lie," said Bloomenback. "You are late in the field; Lucinda and her husband are no more."

"Nay," said Mr. Gage, "Lucinda has dwelt in this house for four years past. It was she who attended upon Mr. Bootle in a serious illness he had last year. Ah! here is Lucinda! the time is come."

With a cry of joy a young female sprang from the door-way and flung herself upon her knees by old Bootle. Oh! how he parted the fair hair upon her brow, and gazed upon her face! How he wept! and then a gentlemanly-looking man advanced to him, and said,—

"Mr. Bootle, I suppose I must introduce myself. I was Lieutenant Brotherton.—I am Colonel Brotherton of the Madras Army. May I call you father?"

"My children! my children!" gasped the old man. "Oh, Heaven! what have I done to deserve to be so happy?"

Bloomenback made a rush from the house, closely followed by Jarvis. They ran against each other in the hall, and struck on each side some heavy blows. Both were full of disappointment. Mrs. Jarvis, the Great Hannibal, J. Gea, Miss Muggins, and Robert Brotherton reached the door in a tumultuous throng. The barouche was there. They clambered in—they held on behind!—they fought—they struggled — the postillions cracked their whips, and away they whirled.

*   *   *   *   *   *

Mr. Bootle lived a good ten years after these events, and a happier party could not be imagined than that which constituted the Old Priory, and made its ancient halls echo again with joyous laughter.

190

The elder Jarvis and Bloomenback disappeared, but Hannibal keeps a little tobacconist's in the City-road; and still now and then, on occasions at the Eagle, Miss Muggins makes an appearance. Selina runs after ladies in Cranbourn-alley —street, we beg its pardon—recommending the last new fashionable bonnet, and her husband is—nobody knows where.

FINIS.

Printed and Published by E. Lloyd, 12, Salisbury-square, Fleet-street.

www.ingramcontent.com/pod-product-compliance
Lightning Source LLC
Chambersburg PA
CBHW080823250626
47160CB00008B/2848